WITHOUT MY BOSWELL

About Hugh Ashton

UGH ASHTON arrived in Japan in 1988 to write manuals for musical instruments and audio equipment, and remained in the country until 2016, when he returned to the UK. He now lives in the Midlands cathedral city of Lichfield with his wife, Yoshiko. He is a member of various Sherlockian societies, and has contributed to the literature on the subject. Rather than the Stradivarius violin played by Sherlock Holmes, he plays a resonator guitar ("Dobro").

Contact him at HAshton@mac.com More details of his books can be found at www.HughAshtonBooks.com.

About Andy Boerger

NDY BOERGER lives in Tokyo, with a family that includes ferrets. He has published several books of his drawings and writings, as well as illustrating other authors' books. He and Hugh Ashton have collaborated on a series of detective stories for children, the first being *Sherlock Ferret and the Missing Necklace*, featuring the world's cutest detective.

His work may be viewed at www.AndyBoerger.com

SOME RECENT COMMENTS ON HUGH ASHTON'S SHERLOCK HOLMES TITLES

"*Hugh Ashton maintains his place as one of the best writers of new Sherlock Holmes stories, in both plotting and style.*" (The District Messenger, *newsletter of the Sherlock Holmes Society of London*)

"*As a (nearly) lifelong fan of Sherlock Holmes, I have received the works about him by modern authors with initial enthusiasm, only to be replaced by disappointment. Such is not the case with Hugh Ashton, who has caught the tone of the original canon perfectly.*"

"I hardly ever give 5 stars to any Sherlock Holmes pastiche because I don't believe that anyone can measure up to the master, A. Conan Doyle, but Hugh Ashton never disappoints me. His stories are always high quality in the style, structure and feel of the originals. I have read too many pastiches to mention and Hugh Ashton's stories would be at the top of the heap."

"Hugh Ashton takes the characters of Sherlock Holmes and Dr Watson back to their origins. I have to admit I am a big Sherlock Holmes fan and have enjoyed the many reincarnations of the character in books, movies and TV series. Hugh Ashton, though, has a more genuine feel and understanding of the original characters, and reading this story I couldn't help feeling a touch of nostalgia for the original Conan Doyle stories."

"One of the blessings of being a senior citizen is being able to be locked into patterns of actions which are simply performed and no explanations provided. One of these is whenever I see another book by Hugh Ashton is simply clicking on it and putting it into the shopping cart."

Without my Boswell: Five Early Adventures of
Sherlock Holmes

Hugh Ashton

ISBN-10: 1-91-260558-9
ISBN-13: 978-1-912605-58-3

Published by j-views Publishing, 2018

This is a work of fiction. Names, characters, places, brands, media, and incidents are either the product of the author's imagination or are written in respectful tribute to the creator of the principal characters.

j-views Publishing, 26 Lombard St, Lichfield, WS13 6DR, UK
publish@j-views.biz www.j-views.biz

DEDICATION – FIRST EDITION (2014)

 HILE this book was in the final stages of preparation, I heard of the sudden death at an early age of a good friend, Kevin Cleary. His kindness and generosity will always stay in my memory, as will the encouragement and practical help he provided to me on so many occasions.

My memories of the things we did and talked about together include delving into the innermost workings of Macintosh computers, discussing US politics as we travelled to Tokyo together on the early morning train (and being told by the other passengers to be quiet about it!), listening to modern country music or talking about 1950s pulp fiction, enjoying a dosa masala at an Indian restaurant, and simply knocking back gin and tonics on a hot Kamakura afternoon. We always seemed to end up striking intellectual sparks off each other, and I, for one, came away from our encounters wiser and better informed.

Kevin, you will be sorely missed. This book is for you and is dedicated to your memory.

Kamakura, 2014

ACKNOWLEDGEMENTS

MY thanks go to all Sherlockians around the world, who encourage me in my writing, and provide a springboard for my imagination. Special thanks to those who have read and suggested improvements to these stories.

Thanks to my friends around the world in every continent. Without you, a writer's life would be very lonely.

Thanks to Andy for his wonderful imagination that expresses itself in his drawings.

And fond memories of Jo and the Beans for their continued belief in me, and their constant support and encouragement.

CONTENTS

HIS volume contains a few words about the author and illustrator (Page iv), a Dedication (Page v) and Acknowledgments (Page vi) as well as a Colophon (Page viii) and a Preface by the author (Page ix), in which some aspects of the stories are explained. The adventures themselves are all referred to by Watson in the works published by him.

" Yes, my boy, these were all done prematurely before my biographer had come to glorify me." He lifted bundle after bundle in a tender, caressing sort of way. "They are not all successes, Watson," said he. " But there are some pretty little problems among them. Here's the *record of the Tarleton murders* (Page 1), and the case of *Vamberry, the wine merchant* (Page 35), and the adventure of the old Russian woman, and the singular *affair of the aluminium crutch* (Page 67), as well as a full account of *Ricoletti of the club-foot, and his abominable wife.* (Page 91)" (from "The Musgrave Ritual")

" I assure you that *the most winning woman I ever knew was hanged for poisoning three little children* (Page 111) for their insurance-money..." (from *The Sign of the Four*)

And at the end of these stories, we invite you to learn more about other books by the same author (Page 143).

COLOPHON

E decided that this adventure of Sherlock Holmes deserved to be reproduced on paper in as authentic a fashion as was possible given modern desktop publishing and print-on-demand technology.

Accordingly, after consulting the reproductions of the original Holmes adventures as printed in *The Strand Magazine*, we decided to use the TT Barrels font as the body (10.5 on 13.2). Though it would probably look better letterpressed than printed using a lithographic or laser method, and is missing old-style numerals, it still manages to convey the feel of the original. The flowers are Bodoni Ornaments, which have a little more of a 19th-century appearance than some of the alternatives.

Chapter titles, are in Amarante, and page headers and footers are in Baskerville (what else can one use for a Holmes story ?), and the decorative drop caps are in Romantique, which preserves the feel of the *Strand*'s original drop caps.

The punctuation is carried out according to the rules apparently followed by the *Strand*'s typesetters. These include double spacing after full stops (periods), spaces after opening quotation marks, and spaces on either side of punctuation such as question marks, exclamation marks and semi-colons. This seems to allow the type to breathe more easily, especially in long spoken and quoted exchanges, and we have therefore adopted this style here.

Some of the orthography has also been deliberately changed to match the original – for instance, " Baker Street" has become " Baker-street" throughout.

PREFACE

 am lost without my Boswell," declares Sherlock Holmes*. Indeed, the interplay between the solid ex-Army doctor, and the more mercurial purveyor of " ineffable twaddle" forms a large part of the appeal of the adventures which Watson caused to be published, and Watson himself, as well as acting as a publicist for Holmes' business, provides more solid assistance on many occasions.

But as I have remarked elsewhere†, Sherlock Holmes would not have allowed himself to associate with a complete dolt. We know that Holmes did not suffer fools gladly, and it would be completely illogical to assume that he would make an exception in the case of Watson. Even so, the two characters complement each other well – Watson is down-to-earth where Holmes may be fanciful ; and while neither man can be accused of physical cowardice, Watson's experiences under fire give him a form of courage which is that of the soldier, rather than that of the adventurer, as displayed by Holmes. It is a mistake to see him merely as a foil for Holmes' wit and intellect. And at the very least, we know

---

*   " A Scandal in Bohemia"
†   " A Defence of John H. Watson", *The Watsonian*, Autumn 2013

him as a raconteur of genius, as he relates the cases of his famous friend, artistically embellishing, withholding, and organising the events he describes in such a way as to capture and hold our imaginations (I take it that no-one reading this is so naïve as to believe that Watson's accounts are plain unvarnished truthful full reports of the adventures he shared with Holmes).

But... before John Watson had that fateful encounter with the eccentric beater of corpses at Barts, there was a consulting detective by the name of Sherlock Holmes, who had already built up a practice and a reputation that extended to Scotland Yard. However much he may have felt lost without his Boswell later in his career, Holmes was playing a solo game when he started out.

We see a little of Holmes alone (apologies for the inevitable pun) in "The Case of the Gloria Scott" and "The Musgrave Ritual", and it is in Watson's account of this latter adventure that we hear of some other cases at a time when Holmes was presumably learning his trade.

The written accounts of some of these were in the dispatch-box, bound together in an envelope, in Watson's writing. The envelope was inscribed "Before My Time", again in Watson's hand.

The stories in here are all somewhat less interesting from the point of view of the interplay between Holmes and other characters, but they all shed a light on Holmes' methods of deduction as he learned his trade, and often also shed light on his character. As Holmes himself remarked, not all of these may be seen as successes, but none of the cases here may be regarded as a complete failure.

S an example of the way in which Holmes' methods were developed, "The Case of the Tarleton Murders" described here gives us not only an insight into his powers of observation and ability to draw conclusions from his observations, but also shows us the psychological tricks that he used in his investigations. But much more than this, it shows the younger Holmes confronted for the first time in his life with a villain of psychopathic intensity. The evil emanating from the wrongdoer seems to have been enough to turn his head, at least temporarily, in the direction of an impulsive action.

Though the relation of the resolution of the case may seem a little rushed at times, we can attribute this to Holmes' emotional state of mind (a rare occurrence indeed!) as he relates this to his friend. There is no doubt in my mind that Watson was well aware of the mental anguish that the recounting of this adventure cost Holmes, and forebore to question him any further on the matter.

HE case of Vamberry, the wine merchant, related by Holmes to Watson, also shows a somewhat different side of the younger Holmes to those displayed in the "Blue Carbuncle" or "The Abbey Grange", for example, in which he allows a confessed criminal to go free. In this case, set in Paris, recorded here, he displays little of the chivalry and compassion that marked the older more experienced detective.

Indeed, the somewhat callous and cavalier attitude that he adopts with regard to the eventual end of one of the villains of this piece (for whom he might be expected to feel some pity, given the circumstances) is very much at odds with the older detective with whom we are more familiar. Are we to conclude, then, that the events Holmes encountered in his work made him more, rather than less, human as he became better acquainted with human frailty ? It is tempting to assume so.

N "The Affair of the Aluminium Crutch", the story talks candidly about Holmes' need for money (which seems to have been somewhat of a concern for him). Here we see a genuine interest in the case and the building up of a new form of business in the younger Holmes, as well as a definite desire to see right and justice prevail.

His interest in science generally, and chemistry in particular, is alluded to here, giving us a more rounded picture of the young detective. It must be realised, though, that this tale is not a verbatim account related to Watson, but has been fleshed out by him from notes furnished by Holmes, and augmented, doubtless, by verbal reminiscences and hints about Holmes' early life and career, possibly not even connected with this case, thrown out from time to time.

HE younger Holmes was not always averse to displaying his more human side, and this is shown in the "The Case of the Abominable Wife", the spouse in question of course, being that of Ricoletti, he of the club-foot. Holmes here shows a touching concern for one whom he has come to regard as a friend, disregarding the rigidity of the class system, and those

prejudices against foreigners that were present in Britain at that time. An interesting sidelight is the value he places on theoretical knowledge gained from books as well as practical knowledge from experience, knowledge which stood him in good stead on this occasion.

In this story of Ricoletti, we see a very human side of the younger Holmes, blessed with the proverbial "champagne tastes" (he would seem to have been somewhat of an epicure) and cursed with the possession of a mere "beer budget". The somewhat tragic ending may surprise the reader a little, as it did Holmes, who would seem to have doubted his own value, or at the least, the value of his profession as a result. It is well for us that he reconsidered his attitude to his chosen profession.

ASTLY, we have "The Adventure of the Two Bottles", a tale of Holmes' student days. Holmes carefully explains to Watson the way in which he built up the evidence, with a number of false starts on his part.

Of particular interest to students of Sherlock Holmes the man (as opposed to Sherlock Holmes the consulting detective) are the hints regarding sexual attraction that he describes himself as feeling. For those who have seen him only as a mere "automaton, a calculating machine", with no interest in the opposite sex, this may come as some surprise. One can only conclude that the older Holmes masked such emotions, as a good Victorian gentleman should.

LL in all, we can see that the younger Holmes was far from being lost without his Boswell. He seems to have been able to take on a number of different cases, and to bring them to satisfactory conclusions, even before he had fully honed his craft.

Without my Boswell

Five Early Adventures of

Sherlock Holmes

From the Dispatch-Box of
John H. Watson MD

Discovered and Edited by

Hugh Ashton

With Five Original Illustrations by
Andy Boerger

THE TARLETON MURDERS

"HE RAISED HIS HEAD, HIS EYES STILL CLOSED, AND I SAW HIS FACE WAS SET IN A RIGID MASK, WITH HIS FISTS CLENCHING AND UNCLENCHING CONVULSIVELY, AS HE DOUBTLESS RELIVED THAT AWFUL SCENE IN HIS MIND."

Editor's Notes

There is no doubt at all in my mind for this adventure's exclusion from the Canon. It is a bloody crime – much more so than those that Watson reported in the canon – and there are elements of sexuality in the crime that would have profoundly shocked and disturbed Watson's readers. Not only would the crime itself have been a reason for secrecy, but Holmes' emotional reaction to the crime would have changed the perception of the great detective from that of a reasoning machine, to a more human personality if it had become known. It is unlikely that Holmes or Watson would have wished this side to become obvious.

This is a "Holmes without Watson" story, and here the foil is Lestrade. Much of Holmes' subsequent relationship with the Scotland Yard detective can be traced from this adventure, where a fragile relationship between the two men is painfully constructed. There is a touching ending to this account that tells us much of the relationship between Holmes and Watson.

Incidentally, this is also an unusual adventure in that it takes place in the North of England – an area seemingly little frequented by Holmes.

T the time that Sherlock Holmes recounted this remarkable tale to me, I was busy with my practice, and had little time to spend with my friend. I confess, though, that I missed the company of this remarkable man, and the excitement that came with being his companion, and my subsequent involvement in his adventures.

However, being at some remove from Holmes, as it were, it struck me that I knew surprisingly little of his character before I had first encountered him, given the depth and strength of our friendship. On my next visit to Baker-street, I ventured to ask him whether he did not find his choice of occupation curiously at odds with the norms of society.

"By no means, my dear Watson," he replied lazily, drawing on his pipe. "I seek to remedy the ills of society in a general sense through analysis and treatment. You do the same, but your field is the individual members of society."

"But have there never been times," I persisted, "when you have felt disgusted, shall we say, at the iniquity of mankind? I confess that there are occasions when my stomach is turned by what I see when I observe my patients' conditions. And more than that, my soul sometimes rebels at the profession I have chosen for myself, when I see some poor helpless sufferer, and I know in my heart that there is nothing I can do for him. Why do I continue? I ask myself. Do not similar feelings affect you on occasion?"

Holmes considered my words for a space, and turned to look at me. "You are right, Watson. There are times when you exhibit more perspicacity than perhaps I give you credit for. Yes, there was indeed one case when my soul was turned, as you put it, and I was almost overcome with black despair at the time. This was the case of the Tarleton murders, which

I think I may have mentioned to you on a previous occasion.[*]
It was a case of passion and revenge, and if I have ever encountered evil in person, it was on that case. If I were to believe in the Devil, I would say that I met him then."

"I was in India at the time," I answered, "but there were
reports of the case in the newspapers, even there. It was indeed a shocking case."

Holmes laughed bitterly. "The newspapers reported only a
half of the facts. Are you ready to hear the other half? Bring
the brandy closer. Here, on this table, and set the glasses
close by. I feel we will both be in need of a restorative by the
time I am through."

"You frighten me," I told him.

"I frighten myself, Watson," he confessed. "The only other
man who knew the whole truth of the matter was an Inspector of the local police, and Lestrade. The former's nerves
were shattered, and he retired from the police force, and
lives, a broken man, in the rural part of Sussex, where he
keeps bees for a living. As for Lestrade – well you know the
man well enough. It is a shadow that will fall over him and
haunt him to the end of his days."

"I am ready, all the same, to hear your story," I said stoutly.

"Good man, Watson. This was at the time when I was
living in Montague-street, and was starting to build up my
practice. Some members of the Metropolitan Police force,
chiefly our friend Inspector Lestrade, had got into the habit of seeking my advice on occasion. Though I accepted no
compensation for these cases, seeing them as a way of hon-
ing my skills, I nonetheless managed to keep body and soul
from drifting too far apart through my taking on private cases. I had no wish to descend to the usual mundane fare of

---

[*]   The case receives a brief mention in "The Musgrave Ritual"

the profession – that is to say, spying on errant spouses – but there was enough work of other more challenging nature to keep me occupied.

"However, it was not a regular business ; by no means as flourishing as the time when I first met you, and we took these rooms here together. I was therefore glad of any interruption that caused me to exercise my mental faculties, and a visit from Lestrade was especially welcome, as I knew it heralded some case which was out of the ordinary, and demanded my particular skills. I had come to value Lestrade as a companion, though not for his intelligence, I assure you."

"For what reason, then ? " I asked.

"Oh, he is not without a certain amount of cleverness, I grant you. But the man is as blind as a mole when it comes to noticing details. He overlooks the most obvious clues. Why, Watson, even you are a perfect Argus with regard to your powers of observation when compared to Lestrade. He completely lacks those powers of imagination and reasoning that are essential to success in the profession. But he is fiercely loyal – to his colleagues, and to his ideas, and to justice, and that bulldog-like tenacity is what has brought him to his current position.

"In any event, it was a pleasing break in the daily routine, such as it was, whenever he came to call on me, and so it transpired on this day that I am describing to you. He came into the rooms at a rush, flung his billycock down upon the couch, and sat down, starting to speak even before he was settled in his chair.

"'My dear Inspector,' I said to him. 'Please take your time. Surely there is nothing in this world that cannot wait the minute that it will take you to catch your breath.' For he was breathing heavily, and his face was flushed with excitement."

"I have noticed a tendency to asthma in Lestrade," I

remarked, "as no doubt have you."

"Indeed so. In any case, he took my advice, and his breathing returned to a more regular state. 'It is murder, Mr. Holmes!' he exclaimed. 'Murder of the most foul and barbaric nature.'

"'I have seen nothing in the newspapers,' I answered him. 'Where is this horror?'

"'In Lancashire, in the village of Tarleton,' he told me. 'The local constabulary are out of their depth, and have requested the help of the Yard.'

"'And you in your turn are out of your depth, and are requesting my help?' I rejoined.

"'Precisely, Mr. Holmes. Of course, I have not seen the scene myself, but it appears to me that your notions, fanciful as they appear at times, might serve to provide us with valuable hints.'"

"Lestrade is never one to acknowledge your successes with the applause they deserve," I remarked, smiling.

"Nor was he ever," said Holmes. "He has mellowed a little with time, but he still seems unwilling to admit that there are smarter men in the business than he. In this case, he passed over a sheet of paper to me. 'This arrived by the first post this morning. It is the preliminary report of the officer of the Lancashire Constabulary in charge of the case. Read it, and let me know what you think.'

"I perused the document, which gave the details of the scene of the crime. As Lestrade had told me, it did indeed appear to be a hideous crime. A Mr. Percy Grimshaw, his wife, Helen, and their two children, Mildred and Peter, aged twelve and eight respectively, had been found dead in the drawing-room by the maid early in the morning. All were in night attire, and all had been horribly cut about the neck, presumably with an axe, the head of which was found in the fireplace. The charred remains of the handle were still attached."

I shuddered. "Indeed, a horrible crime. And the maid discovered them? Did she live in the house? One would assume that such a slaughter as you describe would have attracted her attention, and that of any other servants living in the house."

"An excellent question, Watson. Excellent indeed. She did indeed live in the house, as did the cook and another maid. A groom slept over the stables. None of these had heard anything untoward. The most mysterious part of the whole affair was that the door to the room was locked, and the key was later discovered to be in the lock of the door, on the inside."

"Were the windows also locked?" I asked.

"This was a serious omission from the document. Even Lestrade had noticed this, and he roundly cursed the local force for this oversight. When I had finished reading the report – and there really was very little of value in it other than what I have just told you – I looked up at Lestrade.

"'Well?' said he. 'A train leaves from Euston in forty minutes. We can arrive in Tartleton with changes at Liverpool and Southport, and I have taken the liberty of sending a telegram to the local force and asking them to reserve two rooms for us at a local inn.'

"'Allow me five minutes to collect some items for travel, and I am your man,' I told him. I threw the necessities of daily existence into my Gladstone bag, and picked up the bag I always kept packed with the tools of my trade; the lenses and so on that you have seen me use on many occasions.

"It was a source of some frustration to me that Lestrade knew as little as did I regarding the nature of the victims. Naturally, we could assume that the family was well-to-do, from the number of servants mentioned, but it is always the human touch that makes the difference in these cases. Was the late Mr. Grimshaw a drunkard? A harsh taskmaster? An employer whose employees might bear a grudge against him? In cases like this there is almost always a tempting range of opportunities, but we had no knowledge at this point.

"'Some maniac escaped from an asylum,' said Lestrade, when I asked him for his opinion on the identity of the murderer as we sped towards our destination.

"'There is an asylum nearby?' I asked. 'And reports of an escaped lunatic?'

"'We can make enquiries,' replied Lestrade. 'Surely you must agree that this appears to be the work of a madman?'

"'I agree with nothing of the sort,' I retorted. 'Consider the following. The family was all gathered together in the one room, and they were all reportedly in their nightclothes. This would argue that they had all previously retired for the night. A lunatic such as you describe would have gone from room to room slaughtering his victims in their beds, and he would almost certainly not have spared the servants. I can hardly conceive of your madman assembling his victims in one room in this way. Secondly, the room is described as being locked from the inside. We must ascribe a good deal of cunning to your madman – more than I think is likely. And lastly, the supposed murder weapon, the axe, was thrust into the fire to destroy at least the handle, and presumably to remove any traces of blood, thereby making it harder for you, the police, to present it as evidence in a court case. No, Inspector, I fear that your lunatic will not pass muster.'

"Lestrade considered my words in silence for a few minutes. 'There may well be some truth in your theories, Mr. Holmes,' he admitted. 'But you must admit that it would be remiss if we did not at least consider the possibility and make appropriate enquiries.'

"'By all means do so,' I told him. 'But I fear it will be a sad waste of your time and energy.'

"'Do you have any ideas of your own, then?' he asked me, seemingly nettled at my dismissal of his theory.

"'I have too many theories, and not enough data on which to make a decision. For example, we may take the idea of a suicide as being a possibility, albeit a remote one. The husband finds a pretext to summon the family to one room after they and the servants have retired for the night. He murders them all with an axe, before taking the axe to himself – a difficult, but not impossible contortion – and as his last act thrusts the weapon into the fire.'

"'Impossible!' snorted Lestrade.

"'Highly improbable,' I said, 'but within the bounds of possibility, especially if the arrangement of the bodies and so on supports it.'

"'You have more ideas?'

"'Of course. Who is to say that one of the servants is not responsible, for a reason of which we are currently unaware?'

"Lestrade considered this, and grudgingly admitted that such might be the case.

"'But as yet, I believe it to be impossible for me to make any pronouncement,' I told him, 'since we have yet to visit the scene of the crime. There is, however, one circumstance that particularly intrigues me."

"'And what might that be, Mr. Holmes?'

"'You have the same facts in your possession as do I,' I reminded him. 'There is one point there, in plain view, which should give you pause for thought.'"

I had been following Holmes' narrative with attention, and I broke in at this point. "I believe I know to what you were referring," I exclaimed.

"It is quite possible that you do," Holmes said to me, a faint smile curving his thin lips. "Have the patience to hear me out, and you may then tell me if your deduction was correct or not."

"Very well," I answered him.

"On arrival at the small town of Tarleton, which in truth is little more than a village, we made straight for the small police station, where an Inspector Ruddle, a senior officer of the local force, was waiting for us. Lestrade introduced me as a consultant with some experience in criminal affairs. You must recall that I had no Boswell to sing my praises, and my name was virtually unknown at that time, other than in a rather restricted circle of police and their prey. Though I had dismissed Lestrade's idea of an escaped lunatic, I must credit him with tackling that line of enquiry in a very competent and business-like way. He quickly established that there was a County Lunatic Asylum at Whittingham, on the other side of Preston, not too far away.

"'And have any lunatics escaped?' he asked. Ruddle appeared to be ignorant of any such event, but one of the constables timidly raised his hand.

"'It was in the newspaper two or three days ago that one of the inmates had escaped,' he told us in his thick Lancashire accent. 'One of the most brutal maniacs in the whole of the asylum.' He repeated the details with what appeared to be a certain relish. 'Killed three men with an axe, he did, before they locked him up. The only reason he didn't swing was because he had some doctor who said he was mad, and didn't know what he was doing at the time. Load of blooming rubbish, if you ask me.'

"'Nobody asked you, Stubbings,' replied his superior tartly.

"However, Lestrade thanked him for the information, and

turned to me with a gleam of triumph in his eyes. 'You see, Mr. Holmes, that there is no need for you to spin your fantastic theories. I think we now have the answer to our case. All we have to do is to recapture the madman, and put him back where he belongs.'

"The local officer seemed taken aback by the speed with which Lestrade had disposed of the problem, and blurted an apology to him and to me for having brought us up here on a wild goose chase, as he put it. I, on the other hand, was far from convinced of the truth of Lestrade's supposed solution of the mystery, and expressed my opinion, perhaps with a little more emphasis than was altogether tactful under the circumstances."

I chuckled. "It would not be the first time that you have found yourself in such a position. You and Lestrade are often at odds in your interpretation of events, I have observed."

"Nor have you encountered the last such little fracas, I am sure," Holmes answered me. "In any event, Lestrade seemed more than a little put out by my words, which, as I say, were perhaps expressed with the over-confidence of youth, but assented to my suggestion that we visit the scene of the crime.

"'All has been left as it was originally discovered,' we were assured by Chief Inspector Ruddle. I thanked him for the information, and he and Lestrade and I set off for the scene of the crime, a handsome modern brick villa located a few hundred yards from the police station. On arrival at the house, the front door of which was guarded by a police constable, I stopped and enquired which window was that of the room in which the bodies had been discovered. On being informed of its identity, I approached with my usual caution that I employ on such occasions, and made a minute examination of the ground outside the window, before proceeding to the window itself.

"Lestrade watched me with a certain interest. 'Do you consider the lunatic to have entered through the window, then?' he asked me.

"'Whoever entered the room through the window was no lunatic, especially not of the type we have heard described,' I told him. 'See here.' I pointed to the soft ground, in which it was still possible to discern the prints of feet. 'These, my dear Lestrade, are the prints of hobnailed boots. I do not believe that the inmates of asylums are provided with such footwear. The boots come to the ground under the window, leaving excellent imprints in the soft soil, and it is obvious that the wearer of the boots entered the room through the window. He then exited the room a little later and made his way onto the lawn, where the prints are lost. This much, at least is obvious from even a cursory examination of the evidence.'

"'He might have stolen the boots,' Lestrade remonstrated, but it was obvious that his confidence was somewhat shaken. 'However, I agree with you regarding the direction of the footprints and the fact that the intruder seems to have gained access through the window. Not suicide, then, Mr. Holmes?' he smiled.

"'Suicide would seem to be unlikely, indeed. With regard to your other point, I admit that it is possible for the boots to have been stolen,' I replied. 'However, let us also consider this.' I pointed to a spot on the window-frame where the paint appeared to have been worn away. 'To me, this is clear evidence that the internal catch of the casement was slipped, using some long thin tool, such as this.' I bent in my bag, and retrieved a sliver of steel that I carry for just such purposes. 'See here, as I operate on the next casement, which is identical.' I used the tool on the window, and within ten seconds, I was able to swing it wide. There was a low whistle of surprise from Ruddle behind me.

"'I am glad that you are working with us and not against us, Mr. Holmes,' he said. 'That is as neat a piece of housebreaking as I have encountered in a long while.'

"'My point is not to demonstrate my skills in that area,' I told him. 'Rather, I wish you to examine the mark I have just left on the frame, and the mark we have previously noted on the casement next to it.'

"'Why, they are nearly identical!' exclaimed Lestrade, after a brief inspection.

"'Bless my soul, so they are,' added Ruddle. 'Very good, Mr. Holmes. I think you have proved your point regarding the way in which the room was entered.'

"'More than that, though,' I pointed out. 'I believe this also demonstrates that the intruder was no lunatic. A madman would almost certainly lack the patience or the skill to perform this operation.'

"Lestrade appeared crestfallen at this statement, but rallied with, 'In that case, Mr. Holmes, perhaps you would be good enough to inform us of the identity of the murderer.'

"'That is precisely why you invited me to accompany you, was it not? I propose to fulfil my obligation after we have made a thorough investigation of the scene of the crime.'

"'Very well,' said Ruddle. 'Follow me, please, gentlemen.' He led the way to the front door of the house, and opened a door to a room leading off the hallway. The door-frame had been splintered, and to my eyes, it seemed that the locked door had been forced open. Ruddle followed my gaze.

"'It was the groom, Deegan, who forced open the door, after the kitchen-maid was unable to enter that morning,' he told me.

"It was a horrible sight that met my eyes. There were four corpses, sprawled on the floor, each in a welter of blood. As

Lestrade had told me, the neck of each of the victims had been hacked about by some sharp instrument. I looked closer at the bodies, and was horrified by what I beheld. The night attire of each was in a state of disarray, and the man and his son had been hideously mutilated. I will spare you the full details, Watson, but I am sure your Afghan experiences have made you aware of the reported practices of Afghan women when they capture an enemy."

"Not merely reported," I informed him with a shudder. "I have seen the results of the women's attentions with my own eyes. A private of the Berkshires had been captured by the Pathans, and had escaped after suffering the most unimaginably filthy tortures and deprivations. It fell to me to dress his wounds as best I could, and to console him for the loss of those parts which had been removed. You cannot mean that the same sort of abomination had occurred in this case?"

"The very same," Holmes answered me. "And as for the women..." He paused and buried his head in his hands. "Believe me, I had seen the results of violence before this time, but what I saw there shocked me to the very core. I could not believe what had been done to that poor woman, and that little girl. If I may trouble you for a few fingers of the brandy, Watson?" He raised his head, his eyes still closed, and I saw his face was set in a rigid mask, with his fists clenching and unclenching convulsively, as he doubtless relived that awful scene in his mind.

It was almost unprecedented for Sherlock Holmes to display emotion in this way, and I hastened to supply him with the requested liquor, pouring a small amount for myself. He thanked me, and sipped the drink in silence for a while before continuing.

"We were all taken aback," he said, "and I turned to Lestrade. 'Inspector,' I said to him. 'I believe I owe you an apology. This is indeed the work of a madman, though whether it is he who escaped from the asylum, I still doubt.'

"As I examined the scene with as dispassionate an eye as was possible under the circumstances, I was suddenly struck by a number of facts.

"'What was the weather on the night of the murder?' I asked Ruddle.

"'Why, it was a cold night. A hard frost here, I believe. What has that to do with this business?'

"'Everything,' I told him. 'Observe the feet of the victims. They are bare.'

"'Do you sleep in your boots, Mr. Holmes?' laughed Lestrade sarcastically.

"'I would also draw your attention to the stone floor in the hallway outside this room, and the uncarpeted stairs that I observed as we entered the house.'

"'I begin to catch at your meaning,' said Ruddle.

"'And all of these are in their night attire alone, with no wrapper or dressing-gown,' I pointed out. 'I leave you to draw your own conclusions from this, as well as the fact that there is considerably less blood in this room than I would expect.'

"'More than enough blood for me,' said Lestrade. 'Where is the murder weapon?' Ruddle indicated the fireplace, in which it was possible to discern what appeared to be the head of a small axe.

"'A hatchet, then,' I remarked.

"'So it would appear,' said Ruddle. 'It is just possible to make out what seems to be the ashes of the handle among the clinker of the coal.'

"I bent to the fireplace, and it was indeed as Ruddle had described. The remains of what had been a small hatchet lay there, and it was easy to discern a line of wood ash, which presumably represented the remains of the handle, leading to a blackened axe-head thrust into the fire. A small patch of grey matter by the fender caught my attention. 'Halloa, what is this?' I asked myself aloud, not really expecting an answer.

"'It is ash, such as you might reasonably expect to find in a fireplace,' Lestrade answered me, with a degree of sarcasm still evident in his words.

"'It is not coal ash or wood ash,' I told him. Indeed it was not. I scooped it up and put it into one of the envelopes that I always carry with me. 'I have seen enough in this room,' I told the two policemen. 'For my part, I would strongly recommend photographing the room and the disposition of the bodies before removing them and attempting to restore some dignity to them.'"

Here Holmes again broke off his narrative, and sat silently, sipping the last of his brandy. Without being asked, I refilled his glass, an action he acknowledged with a nod before he spoke again. "I am not, Watson, a sentimental or a superstitious man, as you know. And yet there was something in that room that stirred me. It was the sense of an almost palpable evil at work, which filled me with a pity for its victims. It is an emotion that is typically a stranger to me, and I can provide little explanation for it other than as a reaction to what I had encountered. In any event, we left the room.

"'We should interview the servants,' I told the others. 'In their testimony, I believe that we may discover the truth of this matter.'

"'I have two copies of their statements here,' said Ruddle, handing a thick envelope to Lestrade, and another to me. I read through, but it was obvious that the questioning had been conducted by an officer of limited intelligence, and virtually no imagination. Nonetheless, I managed to produce some words of thanks to Ruddle for his efforts.

"'There are three servants living in the house,' Ruddle reminded us. 'The cook, Mrs. Dolan, a scullery-maid, Betty Cartwright, and a parlour-maid, Lily Minton.'

"'And a groom living over the stables,' Lestrade reminded him. 'James Deegan may well have seen or heard something of the intruder, and it was he, was it not, who first broke down the door and discovered the bodies.'

"'Indeed so. Whom shall we call in first?' asked Ruddle.

"'The cook, if you have no objections,' I requested. It is my habit when questioning a household, Watson, always to start with the most senior of the servants. Following their interview, they are typically less likely to gossip in the servants' hall than the younger more junior members of the household, such as the maids or the boots and so on. In that way, if the culprit is to be located among the servants, there is less chance of an advance warning of the subjects and nature of the expected interview from those who have previously been questioned. It is by no means an infallible system, but it typically serves me well.

"As it turned out, the others had no objection to this suggestion of mine, and Mrs. Dolan presented herself before us in due course. By tacit consent, it was I who posed most of the questions to her. In answer to the question as to whether she had heard anything on the fatal night, her answer was an unequivocal negative.

"'I have trouble sleeping,' she told us, and I usually take several drops of laudanum before I go to bed, sir. That helps me sleep like a baby until it's time to get up.' I had remarked the tell-tale signs of one addicted to opium before she had informed us of this, but it was good to have this confirmed by the woman herself. Her room, it appeared, was on the top floor, at the other end of the house from that of the room in which the bodies were lying, and even without the laudanum, it is hard to see how she could have heard anything untoward.

"When asked about the character of her late employers, she had nothing but praise for Mrs. Grimshaw, and for the two children, whom she described as 'perfect angels', but she appeared to be somewhat reticent about the husband. She would only say that 'he paid me my wages on time, and always ate what was put in front of him'. It seemed to me that there was very little use in questioning her further.

"Before she left, I asked her if there was anything at all unusual that she could remember about the evening of the night on which the murders had taken place. She paused and frowned. 'Actually, now that you mention it, yes, there was something funny there, sir. I started a new bottle of laudanum only four or five nights ago. The bottle should have been almost full, but it is nearly empty now, and it was nearly empty on the night that they all were killed.'

"'Thank you,' I told her, making a note. 'You are sure that the bottle emptied on that night?'

"'Yes, sir, there is no question about it at all in my mind. As clear as I am talking to you now.' She left the room, and I felt that another piece of the puzzle had fallen into its appointed place.

"'Betty Cartwright, the scullery-maid next, I think,' I said. She turned out to be a middle-aged woman, who told us that she had worked for the Grimshaw household for seven years.

"'A very contented family, for the most part. She was a good mistress, and the children were little darlings,' was all she would say about her late employers, refusing to provide any further details. Again, it was unlikely that she would have heard anything, given the location of her bedroom. She told us that she had retired to bed with a headache.

"'It was you, was it not, who discovered the bodies?' I asked her.

"'Not as such," she answered. It was me who found the door was locked, and I called up to the stables to Deegan to come and break it down, as the master and mistress didn't answer when I knocked on their bedroom doors. He came down and forced the door open. And there they all were, in a pool of blood. Oh, it was horrible. I fainted, I tell you, and when I came to, I was in the kitchen. Deegan had carried me there, and sat me in a chair. And then Mrs. Dolan took care of me while Deegan went for the police. Lily – that's the parlourmaid – was out for the night. Her sister's child had taken sick, and she had received permission to help her sister care for the baby. She came in when I was in the kitchen. We told her what had happened, and what we had seen.'

"'What was her reaction?' I asked.

"'I suppose you would say it was what you would expect. Mind you, I wasn't taking much notice of other people at that time. I was all of a flutter myself, and the world was spinning round me, if you know what I mean, sir."

"'Why were you attempting to enter the drawing-room?' Lestrade asked her.

"'That's my job, sir. I look after all the fires in the house, and I was there to clean out the ashes from the night before.'

"'So the fire was burning all night? Is that not somewhat dangerous?'

"'Burning all night, sir? Not at all. It's my job to clean out the ashes and lay the fires in the morning, and to make sure they're all out when the family goes to bed. Except for the ones in the master's and mistress's bedrooms, that is. They take care of putting them out for themselves.'

"As you can imagine, Watson, this information was of great interest to me. 'You are sure that the fire in the drawing-room was out when you went to bed?' I asked her.

"'Absolutely sure, sir. I made sure that the fire was

properly out and there was no unburned coal left in the grate, and then shut the drawing-room door, and used the key to lock it. I'd take my oath on that.'

" ' You may have to do exactly that,' remarked Lestrade quietly.

" ' But I didn't do anything, sir,' she protested.

" ' We know that,' I told her, 'but the words of a sensible woman such as yourself will be of great value in helping determine what really happened. You have been of great help here.' Her face lit up at these words of praise, and I followed my line of questioning. 'The key was in the lock of the door, on the inside ? '

" ' So Deegan said to me. I never saw it myself. The door was definitely locked, though, sir.'

" ' Excellent, Betty. You are obviously not in the habit of inventing stories, and you only report what you know to be true and what you have seen with your own eyes.'

" ' That's the way I was brought up, sir, and there's nothing going to change that.'

" We dismissed her, and I told Lestrade and Ruddle that in my opinion the man Deegan should be the next to be questioned. They offered no objection, and a surly-looking man, aged between thirty and forty, with a strong whiff of the stables about him, entered the room.

" Without waiting for us to speak to him first, he burst out with the words, ' I don't know anything about it. I was asleep over the stables as always, and I knew nothing until Betty came knocking on the door and woke me up.'

" ' Thank you, that is most helpful,' I told him, in an attempt to gain his confidence a little. ' Let me ask you a few questions, if I may, regarding the state of the room when you broke open the door.' He reluctantly gave his assent, but it was difficult for me to gain any clear picture of what had occurred when he saw the interior of the room. He claimed to have been overcome with horror at the sight, the truth of which statement I was inclined to credit. Subsequent to this, he corroborated the scullery-maid's account, saying that he had picked her up and carried her to the kitchen, where he had attempted to revive her.

"'Was the fire in the fireplace burning when you opened the door?' Lestrade asked him at one point, displaying an acuteness that somewhat surprised me.

"'I couldn't tell you that, sir,' he mumbled. 'It wasn't something you'd notice, really, given the other things there.'

"'I am sure that is true,' I assured him. 'May I ask you a few more questions about your work here?' It appeared that Deegan had worked in the household for several years. As well as being the groom, he also was responsible for some of the rough outdoor work in the garden, as well as some of the heavier fetching and carrying of coal for the stove and fireplaces, sacks of potatoes and the like. When questioned about his relationship with the family, he provided a similar answer to those of the cook and the scullery-maid, that is to say, that he praised the mistress of the household, and her children. A noticeable scowl spread over his face when he mentioned Mr. Grimshaw, but he told us that 'he was a fair employer to me', though the words sounded somewhat forced to my ears.

"'By the by,' I said to him as he was leaving, 'I see by the bulge in your pocket that you are a pipe-smoker.'

"'So I am,' he answered me. 'What of it?'

"'It is nothing; a mere trifle. I too am a devotee of the weed, but I find I have come down from London without my tobacco-pouch. Would it be too much to ask if I could call on your lodgings above the stables in a little while and purchase some tobacco from you?'

"He laughed. 'No need for the money. I'll gladly share with another man who loves his tobacco. Now if you want to know something more about the master, it's that he couldn't abide the smell of tobacco. I could never smoke in his presence, and of course in a stable, you have to be careful of fire. I'll gladly give you a fill, officer, if you step up to see me. I'll be there for the next thirty minutes or so, at least.' So saying, he left the room.

" 'No love lost there between man and master,' remarked Ruddle. 'More than his pipe involved there, I would say.'

" 'I agree,' I said. 'But before I collect my tobacco – and I thank you, Lestrade, for not mentioning the fact that I do in fact have my tobacco with me, as you saw for yourself on the train coming down – we must talk to Lily, the parlour-maid, who was not in the house that night, according to what we have been told.'

"Lestrade chuckled. 'I know why you have so conveniently forgotten your tobacco. Ruddle here or I would require a warrant to enter his lodging. You amateurs have powers denied to us poor official guardians of the law.' He opened the door and called for Lily Minton.

"I do not know what we were expecting to enter the room, Watson, but it certainly was not the feminine vision that presented itself to us in the shape of the parlour-maid. I lack your connoisseurship in these matters," he smiled at me, " but I have rarely seen a female form that would appeal more to the majority of men."

"But not to you ?" I could not refrain from asking.

"The features were all those that an artist could wish for, should he wish to paint a portrait of Venus. The figure, such as could be discerned under the servant's dress, could have been the model for a classical statue. And yet... There was something missing behind the eyes. True beauty comes from within, and what was within in this instance was far from beautiful. Even so, the effect of her face and her figure was sufficient to cause both Lestrade and Ruddle to become virtually tongue-tied in her presence. As for me, even I can confess that I found her disconcerting. There may not have been what you or I would term intelligence there, but there was a certain amount of cunning apparent from the set of her lips, and the way that her eyes darted around the room.

"She answered our questions readily enough, though, telling us that she had served the family with their dinner of curried mutton, followed by a treacle sponge pudding, before leaving the house. Rather than her sister's child which was ill, as we had been told previously, she told us that it was her cousin who had a sick baby. But such discrepancies do occur in cases, where details are remembered wrongly or become confused in the turmoil of events, and I felt this could be regarded as being irrelevant to our enquiries.

"She told us that that she had returned to the house to find Deegan standing over an unconscious Betty in the kitchen, with Mrs. Dolan in a state of some panic at the news that Deegan had apparently just imparted. Other than that, she said that she could tell us no more of the terrible events of that night.

"When asked about her relationship with her employers, she answered that she had no time for the family, and indeed had intended to give in her notice that week, on the grounds that she found it impossible to work there, but refused to give more details.

"'We will probably be asking you more questions later,' Ruddle told her before dismissing her. 'Well,' he said, turning to Lestrade and me as the door closed behind her. What do we have here?'

"Lestrade looked at me, and taking my cue, I began. 'We

have a series of paradoxes. We have a fire which was out and then was relighted. We have a door which was locked from the outside, and then was unlocked and relocked from the inside. This despite clear evidence that an intruder entered the room through the window.'

" 'These are the reports of one person alone,' pointed out Lestrade.

" 'That is so, but I happen to know that this Betty Cartwright attends the same chapel as do I myself, and I have never heard ill spoken of her,' said Ruddle. 'I feel we can trust her testimony, unscientific as my opinion may appear to you London men. Pray continue, Mr. Holmes.'

" 'We have a barbaric crime committed, which reminds me of nothing so much as those vile practices that Eastern women inflict upon their captives,' I said to the others. 'And we have in the household a man who has served in the Indian Army. No? You failed to observe the darkened skin and the bearing typical of one who has served as a soldier, not to mention the Oriental style of his cravat-pin? Well, let that pass, as well as the fact that you apparently failed to notice that he was wearing hobnailed boots of a pattern seemingly identical to those which produced the prints outside the window. Not only has he served as a soldier, by the way that he carries himself and from his manner, I would lay odds that he was the victim of the cat on more than one occasion.'"

"Those floggings that I witnessed were terrible affairs," I said to Holmes. "I never knew any good to come of them. Usually the culprit went from bad to worse, and often ended up being hanged."

"And so it was here," said Holmes. "But I leap ahead of myself. As I explained to the others, I intended to use the borrowing of some tobacco at least to gain a glance at the interior of his room. I had another object in mind, which I did not reveal at the time.

"'What about the maid Minton?' asked Lestrade.

"'Well, what of her?' I asked.

"'She is the only one of the servants to speak ill of the late Mrs. Grimshaw,' pointed out Ruddle.

"'Perhaps Mrs. Grimshaw had reason to speak ill of her. I have strong suspicions by now,' I replied. 'But I will know more when I have returned from the local public house.'

"'What?' exclaimed Lestrade. 'What will you do there, in heaven's name?'

"'I intend to spend my time enjoying a pint or two of good Lancashire ale to accompany the tobacco that I am now about to acquire,' I told them, and left the house to make my way to the stables.

"Deegan opened the door to my knock, and was affable enough in handing over a screw of tobacco, but there was a look of wary caution hidden behind the smile he gave me. While the door was open, I was able to see one or two items which were of great interest to me. As I took the offered tobacco, I remarked that I had heard good things about Lancashire brews, and asked if he could recommend a local hostelry where I might sample them. He appeared very willing to oblige me in this matter, and directed me to the Legh Arms, a little outside Tarleton, towards Stockport, an establishment which he told me he frequented often enough, and could recommend from his experience. This was not, by the way, the inn in which Lestrade and I were expecting to stay. By a strange coincidence, I would have to pass through a hamlet by the name of Holmes to reach it.

"I set off on my quest, and found the inn as described. The bar was full of talk of the murders, a few rumours of which had escaped and were being talked about in hushed whispers. Happily the more bloody details were absent. When it was learned that I was from London, it was immediately assumed that I was a newspaper reporter, a misapprehension which I did nothing to dispel.

"The purchase of a few drinks loosened some tongues, and words were soon flying about Jimmy Deegan and his late employer. As I had surmised, there was a lot of salacious talk about the parlour-maid Lily Minton and Grimshaw. Apparently he had the reputation of having had a roving eye, and it was widely put about that not a few of the younger members of the Tarleton population were his offspring. Talk had been going around for some time about him and the maid.

"'And that really annoyed Deegan, that did,' my informant told me, drinking the beer I had bought him. 'He came in here one night, fighting mad, and said that his Lily had tried to fight off Grimshaw, but he had forced himself on her. Deegan reckoned Lily was his girl, you know that? They were saving up to leave this town and go and live quietly somewhere. He told me one evening some things about his past. He said he'd done some bad things in his time in India when he was a soldier, and the feelings still came over him sometimes, but he was now trying to lead an honest and God-fearing life, and with the help of a good woman, he'd get things right.' I have to admit that, based on my observations of Minton, I would not describe her as a 'good woman', but I let that pass.

"'Why did she not leave the household?' I asked.

"'She wanted to stay with Deegan, he said.' The old man shook his head. 'Women,' he said bitterly. 'I don't think we'll ever understand them.' I laughed at his words, and nodded my agreement before leaving the tavern and making my way back to Tarleton.

"By now, as you will have surmised, I had the solution to the case. Deegan was undoubtedly the murderer, and he had almost certainly been assisted by Minton, seeking revenge for the outrage perpetrated on her by her employer."

"I can see that Deegan had the motive," I said to Holmes, "but I cannot see how he managed to lure the family downstairs in their nightclothes and then proceed to butcher them."

"He did no such thing," Holmes replied. "Let me tell you of the remainder of the tale, and I can then explain how it was that the crime was committed. It was a crime of some ingenuity and much emotion and had been some time in the planning, though the timing of the execution was dependent on other events. I returned to the police station where I had arranged to meet Ruddle and Lestrade, and I placed my findings before them. At the end of my explanation, they both agreed that Deegan should be arrested immediately without further delay.

"'You will need several burly constables,' I warned them. 'He is a strong man, and a desperate one.'

"'Will you join us?' asked Lestrade.

"'I would prefer not to be present at the arrest. If you feel my presence would be valuable when he is brought in, I will be with you.'

"They left in the company of three or four constables, and returned about thirty minutes later, bringing with them a handcuffed and struggling Deegan.

"Lestrade called me into the room while he was formally charged with the murder of the Grimshaw family, and his statement was being taken. At the sight of me, his face convulsed with rage and hate. I have never seen a face turn almost black with anger, save on this occasion, and I confess to being frightened. I was in no physical danger, you understand. Deegan was handcuffed, and supported by two large well-trained constables. I was on the other side of a large deal table, and I am well able, as you know, to defend myself. No, what was frightening was the overwhelming impression that I was in the presence of a force of almost elemental evil.

"He freely admitted to the slaughter of the family, and it was no consolation to me at all that my deduction of the case corresponded point for point with his description of the events of that terrible night. He told his tale with a kind of fierce glee, seemingly proud of the evil he had wrought, spitting out his words with a proud defiance.

"At one point, when he laughingly told of the mutilations he had carried out on the children and their parents, I could no longer restrain myself. I stood up and went close to him, raising my hand to strike him down. I do not believe Lestrade or Ruddle would have stopped me. They, too, were horrified and shocked by what they were hearing. However, I stayed my hand, and I did something which was in many ways worse than merely striking him, and for which I have never been able to fully forgive myself."

He paused, and mopped his brow, seemingly overcome by the memory. "What on earth could you do?" I asked.

"I spat at him. Full in the face, several times. It was an abominable thing for me to do, even to a man such as Deegan. Immediately I had done it, I knew I had done wrong, but I could find no words to apologise. Instead, I simply turned and walked out of the room, and out of the police station to the inn where Lestrade and I were booked. I collected my bags, and caught the first train back to London, away from that terrible town.

"And that, Watson, is the tale of my part in the Tarleton murders. The whole truth of the matter was never made public."

"But how did you solve the case?" I asked.

"Oh, that was absurdly simple. I was slow and careless in

my thinking."

"It was at the start of your career," I reminded him.

"There are no excuses for incompetence, Watson. There were so many clues. First of all, it was assumed that the family had been murdered in the room where the bodies were found, and that they had entered the room of their own accord. Obviously, that was not the case. None was wearing a gown or wrapper over their night clothes, and none was wearing slippers, though it was a cold night, and the floor of the hallway was composed of stone flags. In any event, what could have brought them together in one room like that?"

"I have no idea," I said.

"The answer is who it was who brought them together, not what. Let me reconstruct events for you. When Minton left the house, she went, not to her relative's, but to her lover living above the stables.

"The whole affair grew out of Grimshaw's assault on the girl, then?"

"Indeed it did. It transpired that she was with child. It was this fact that saved her from being hanged following her arrest and trial. She claimed that the unborn child was Grimshaw's. When she told Deegan of her condition, his anger, never far from the surface, began to rise up, but it was a cold calculating kind of anger – the most pernicious kind.

"The timing of the atrocious deed was determined by the news that an axe-wielding lunatic had escaped from the local asylum. This news no doubt also determined his modus operandi to some extent.

"Before Minton left the house, she had used the laudanum previously stolen from the cook to drug the family's evening meal. It is quite possible that the dose administered in their food was a fatal one. Curried mutton would disguise any taste of the drug. The family retired, and entered a heavily drugged state. Possibly death ensued as a result, especially in the case of the children, but in any event, the family members would be comatose and close to death.

"You will remember that I had remarked that the blood was less than I would expect? In other words, the axe wounds and mutilations were carried out on corpses, or on near-corpses. Once the family had been drugged, Deegan carried them down the stairs, one at a time, and placed them in the drawing-room. He freely admitted to having carried the other maid to the kitchen after she fainted, after all. His strength was easily up to the task."

"But how did he enter the house? Through the window?"

"Yes, but I could not work out why at the time. Lestrade told me, though, that in Deegan's later statement he added that he had carried a sack of coal to start the fire in the fireplace, and it seemed more discreet if this entrance was carried out through the window before his confederate, Minton, slipped into the house through the back door, to which she had been entrusted with a key. Once he was inside and the fire was started, she unlocked the door of the room from the outside, and Deegan was free to carry the dead or dying bodies of the family to the drawing-room. He then did his horrible work, which was in part revenge for the wrongs that he felt he had suffered at the hands of his employer – he provided a long list of such in his statement – partly as a way of ensuring that the victims were indeed dead, and not merely in a drugged state. And partly, of course, to lead the investigation in the direction of the escaped madman."

"And the purpose of the fire? I had previously noted during your account that a fire seemed to have been left alight after the family had retired for the night. This was the point that you noted when Lestrade first gave you the report in London?"

"Well done, Watson. Yes, that was the point that struck me. As to the purpose of the fire, it was twofold, at the least. First, he wished to dispose of the grisly remains of his butchery. This is as certain as it may be. No trace of those parts removed from the bodies has been discovered. Also, he wished to dispose of the axe he used, which could easily be traced to him. When I called on him for the tobacco, I noticed a set of tools hanging on the stable wall, precisely arranged, with an obvious gap in the arrangement. The way that the paint had faded in parts exposed to the sunlight showed me that the missing tool was a hatchet. There was also hanging there, by the way, a broad-bladed bricklayer's trowel, which could have been used to open the window. It is also possible that even a murderer such as Deegan wished to provide for his own comfort and that of his lover. It was a cold night, after all."

"I take it that the strange ash that you discovered in the grate was from Deegan's tobacco?"

"Naturally. As you know, I have made a study of the subject, and have contributed a monograph where I clearly identify the differences between one hundred and forty types of ash. By obtaining a sample of his tobacco for myself, I was able to confirm that it was he who had entered the room. In addition, by the by, I observed standing on a table in his room, a photograph of Minton. It was clear to me, even before my visit to the Legh Arms, that there was some kind of relationship between the two."

"The door locked with the key on the inside? I can see that Deegan may have escaped through the window, but the maid, Lily Minton?"

"What we were told is that, as you say, Deegan left the room through the window. Minton then fastened the window, and left the dreadful chamber through the door, locking it behind her and pocketing the key. She left the house through the back door, locking that also, and returned to the room above the stables where she passed the key to her lover.

"He was almost certain to be called to break down the drawing-room door, and it was the work of a moment for him to slip the key into the lock on the inside, after he had broken into the chamber, and the scullery-maid had fallen senseless at the sight of the mutilated bodies.

"As to my actions in the police station, I am almost inclined to show leniency in the case of a murderer whose victim has provoked him or her, and who has killed in a sudden flash of rage. But for killers such as Deegan and Minton, who plot and plan, and execute their plans ruthlessly and with a deadly efficiency... Ah, I have no words I can use. Perhaps it was the fact that I could not express my feelings that caused me to behave as I did.

"The fear and loathing that I continue to experience when I recall the Tarleton murders is not just directed at the crime and its perpetrators. It is, if I am to be honest with you, partly directed at myself, and those parts of my nature that perhaps I have no wish to acknowledge." He sank into a moody silence which lasted for a good ten minutes, during which time I sat silently. "Forgive me, my friend. I have said too much, and it is unjust of me to lay my burdens upon you in this way. It is good of you to be so patient with a fool such as myself."

I protested that he was no fool, and in being with him and hearing his thoughts I was doing no more than discharging my duties as a friend.

"Be that as it may, Watson," he said, cheering a little, " perhaps some music would serve to settle our spirits ? Forgive my bungling of the Chaconne from Bach's Second Partita." So saying, he took up his Stradivarius, and with a dreamy half-smile on his lips, brought forth sublime music, his previous troubles seemingly forgotten.

THE CASE OF VAMBERRY THE WINE MERCHANT

"...ONE NIGHT AS WE SAT QUIETLY SIPPING A
FINE OLD BRANDY; A GIFT, HE TOLD ME, FROM A
CERTAIN EUROPEAN FAMILY OF INTERNATIONAL
RENOWN, THE HEAD OF WHICH HE HAD RECENTLY
ASSISTED IN A MATTER OF GREAT DELICACY."

EDITOR'S NOTES

This adventure of Sherlock Holmes before he met John Watson seems to have various links to the canonical stories as published by Watson in his lifetime. Certainly, the French detective Le Villard appears in The Sign of the Four. The case of Vamberry is mentioned in "The Musgrave Ritual", of course, and it is now quite certain, from Watson's note, that the extra income to which Holmes refers in this tale is the result of work undertaken for the British government at the behest of Mycroft. It is also likely that this adventure formed the basis of Holmes' closer relationship with the French police, as hinted at in "The Golden Pince-Nez".

Because it is Holmes himself telling the story, the observation and deductions that mark Watson's recounting of the cases are largely absent. As Watson remarks, Holmes is typically modest about his abilities. Nonetheless, we do gain some idea of the younger Holmes – an accomplished linguist, in French at least – with a love of disguise, and a sense of dramatic timing that is apparent in many of the "Watson" cases. Also of note is Holmes' ability as a connoisseur of fine wine. Though we have previously been aware to a certain extent of Holmes' appreciation of good food and drink, this is a slightly new twist to our knowledge of the character of the great detective.

T was not Sherlock Holmes' custom to take an ostentatious pride in his successes. Indeed, I became aware of many of his more interesting cases only after some time, and it is quite possible that he was a participant in many adventures of which I am still unaware.

At the time that he related the case which I have recorded as "The Musgrave Ritual", he mentioned the records of a few other cases that he had stored in an old tin box. Among these was the story of Vamberry, the wine merchant, a tale which is of considerable interest, though the circumstances were in no way as dramatic as those of some of the other cases in which he was involved.

He related it to me after dinner one night as we sat quietly sipping a fine old brandy; a gift, he told me, from a certain European family of international renown, the head of which he had recently assisted in a matter of great delicacy.

"I can never see such a bottle of fine Napoleon brandy," he remarked, "without being reminded of the events surrounding the wine merchant, Vamberry. It was a case before your time, Watson, when I was still learning my trade, and dividing my time between the British Museum's Reading Room to gain a better theoretical understanding of those matters pertaining to my trade, and walking the streets of London to improve my practical knowledge."

"Ah, yes," I answered him. "I seem to remember your mentioning the case in the past, but you never provided the details."

"That was because I was under an obligation not to divulge them while the principals in the case were still alive. I saw in the newspapers last week that the last of them had now died, and I am now at liberty to entertain you with the case, if you should so wish."

"Of course I am curious about the matter," I said, and poured a little more of the noble amber liquor into our glasses.

Holmes took his glass, thanked me, and commenced his tale. "I was at the time living in Montague-street. There was little in the way of interesting cases to occupy me, and I had yet to establish those relations with Lestrade and the other Scotland Yard detectives that have proved so fruitful a source of recercé problems. Do you know," he laughed, "I had even thought of taking a position as a lawyer's clerk, if only to keep body and soul together."

"There might have been other benefits. It would also have given you some deeper experience of the law and of legal matters," I pointed out.

"Indeed it would have done, and that was one reason that the idea commended itself to me," he agreed. "However, happily for me, and possibly happily for the legal profession, it was not to be. I received a knock on the door of my rooms one morning, and opened it to discover a somewhat agitated gentleman with his fist raised, ready to knock again. From his dress, I concluded that he was not a fellow-countryman, a suspicion that was confirmed as soon as he opened his mouth to speak.

"'You are Monsieur Holmes?' he asked me, with a pronounced French accent. 'The detective?'

"As you are aware, Watson, I have French blood, and it had been the fancy of my parents, when I was a schoolboy, to send me to France where I spent the summers with my French relations. As a result, my knowledge of the French tongue was extensive, though it had been some years since I had occasion to converse at length using it. Nevertheless, it was in that language that I replied to him, informing him that indeed this was the case, and inviting him to enter.

"Once he was inside and comfortably ensconced in the only armchair in the room – Watson, you would scarcely credit how meanly those rooms were furnished – he proceeded to identify himself and tell me his story. We continued to converse in French, which appeared to please him not a little, as he puffed out his chest and told me about himself, not without a certain amount of pride which I secretly found to be comic.

"He was a M. Duclasse, attached to the French Legation here in some capacity that he did not name, but hinted strongly that he was connected with the Sûreté, which as you know, is the detective branch of the French national police force.

"'We have a problem,' he told me, 'of a most delicate and complex nature. It may seem a trifling matter to you, but believe me, it is a serious matter for the Republic. You may not be aware that the President of our nation is a connoisseur of the fine things of life? Food, wine, women... well, maybe we need not dwell on that last. It is with the second that we are most concerned. Some years ago, a certain gentleman residing in the region of the town Cognac was fortunate enough to encounter some cases of brandy that had been deposited there many years before. This brandy was of the cru we know as Grande Champagne, and, according to the labels on the outside of the case, had been destined for the table of the great Emperor, Napoleon Bonaparte himself.

"'The date given on the labels on the cases of these bottles?' he continued, with that shrug of the shoulders which is so characteristic of our French cousins. "The year was 1815, that of the Battle of Waterloo, which you doubtless recall as an English victory from your history lessons at school. Of course in France, we regard it otherwise.' He shrugged again. '*C'est la vie, non*? It is clear that the merchant who had packed these bottles ready for dispatch to his Emperor had found it unnecessary, or maybe unprofitable, to continue with the transaction.'

" ' In any event, our worthy discoverer of the cases, being no fool, realised what a treasure he had discovered. I do not refer, naturally, to merely the monetary value of the brandy, but to the gastronomic riches contained in these bottles. He took the liberty of opening one to determine for himself the true worth of his find, and confirmed his ideas as to its value.

" ' Knowing as he did the value that the President of our Republic places on such things, he offered the remainder of his find to the Élysée Palace, for a suitable consideration. Although our worthy bourgeois is a true patriot and lover of his country, he wished to be compensated adequately for his patriotism. You understand ?

" I replied that I did, and asked, as a matter of some interest, the amount that had been paid for this brandy. The answer came as a considerable surprise to me. I cannot recall the exact amount, but I remember calculating with some amusement that I could have maintained myself for a number of years in the style in which I was currently living with the sum he named.

" ' But you did not come to me to discuss old brandy,' I said to him.

" ' Indeed I did," he retorted. ' That is precisely why I am here. Let me inform you of the events of a week ago. Our Ambassador here in London was invited to dinner with one of your noblemen.' Here he named the peer in question, a Lord ____*. ' Following the dinner, which he reports was of the usual standard of English cuisine – that is to say, virtually

---

*   Note by Watson : Since the descendants of the noble lord still occupy a prominent position in the public life of this nation, though the man himself died some time ago, I have determined not to name him.

inedible – his host presented him with a glass of brandy, the like of which he had only tasted once or twice previously. Those occasions were at the Élysée Palace. Astounded that brandy of this quality should have made its way to these shores, he enquired of his host if he might be permitted to examine the bottle. Such permission being granted, he was astonished to see that it was identical to that which he had previously enjoyed in Paris.'

" 'You suspect Lord ___ to have purloined the brandy from your President ? ' I smilingly asked the Frenchman.

" ' No, no, no, and again no. Of course I am accusing him of no such thing,' protested my visitor. 'But it is important for me to find out the source of this brandy. Simply consider for yourself ! If the thief can obtain something as priceless as this cognac, you must imagine what else could be the target. Treaties. Secret papers. Anything ! ' He spread his hands wide in a gesture of defeat. I had to smile to myself once again at the idea of conflating the importance of brandy with that of government treaties."

" I wonder what your brother Mycroft would have made of that comparison ? " I laughed.

" Brother Mycroft would have maintained his decorum, of that I am sure," answered Holmes, " but I am sure that his inward reaction would be the same as mine. In any event, my next speech was a simple one, which I was sure would answer the question before him.

" 'Why, the answer is perfectly simple,' I said to him. 'The worthy citizen who made the original discovery kept some bottles in reserve, possibly as some kind of insurance against a rainy day. He has sold these extra bottles, probably to some itinerant English dealer in wines and spirits, and is now consoling himself with the contents of those bottles of inferior quality which he has purchased with the proceeds.'

"'My dear M. Holmes,' my visitor admonished me. 'I would have hoped that you had a higher opinion of the police forces of France than this. This was the first thought that occurred to me, and I sent off a telegram to my superiors in Paris immediately I was apprised of the situation. They in turn telegraphed the authorities in the town of Cognac, and our worthy citizen was interrogated by them about the brandy he had discovered. He vigorously denied that there had ever been any bottles other than those he had supplied to the President, other than the one he had opened and sampled for himself. He swore this to be the truth, and our agents had no choice but to believe his words.'

"'Then,' said I, 'there is one more possible explanation. The hoard that your citizen presented to your President was not the only one of its kind. Another has been discovered and smuggled out of the country to here, where a favoured few have been allowed to purchase it.'

"Again my interlocutor shook his head. 'M. Holmes, I am sorry to tell you that the reports I had received of your intelligence appear to be sadly mistaken. You cannot seriously believe that this was not imagined by us, can you? Naturally, this possibility had also been carefully considered by our agents in Paris. As you may imagine, a most careful inventory is maintained of those bottles in the Élysée Palace. On examination of the stocks in the cellar there, it was discovered that all the cases which contained the bottles were present, but that one whole case which should have been full was completely empty! All the bottles had been taken from it – a dozen in all.' He paused, and wiped his brow with his handkerchief. 'The conclusion is obvious, M. Holmes. The brandy was abstracted from the Palace at some time in the past six months. That much is certain, since a careful inventory of the cellar was made then, and all the cases and their contents were listed. Now we know that least some of the missing contents of the empty case have made their way over the Channel to this country. That much is also certain.'

" 'And you would wish me, as an Englishman who is not connected with the official police, to make enquiries in this country as to how this came about, and to identify the culprit responsible, and whether he is currently in England or in France ?'

" 'Precisely, M. Holmes. You may go where I may not. As a Frenchman, even as an official representative of the French Republic, I would have little access to those areas of society where you may enter freely. I am sure that you have your own ideas of how and where you may start your investigations, but if it were up to me, I would begin by questioning the noble lord's servants and making demands of them as to the source of the brandy.'

" 'Then we are of one mind, on this at least,' I told him. There then came, Watson, the part of my business for which I have always felt some distaste. That is to say, the agreement as to my fee. In this particular instance, given that my client was a large and prosperous government, I felt little compunction about demanding a large sum for my labours. Somewhat to my surprise, this demand was met with no opposition, and I felt I had seriously undervalued my services in this case."

"It has always remained somewhat of a mystery to me," I said to my friend, "how you determine the fees for your services. I do not pretend to know the exact details of your finances, but it seems to me that your expenditure exceeds your income, and I have never heard you talk of private means."

"There is some truth in what you say," he agreed, laughing. "It is true that I lack private means, but there is a source of income that I have never disclosed to you, but must, for various reasons, remain a secret from the public. If I tell you that my brother acts as the paymaster, perhaps you will have some idea of the work that I perform that earns this money."

I had a vague understanding of the kind of activities to which he was referring, but refrained from comment.†

Holmes continued, "When my visitor had left me, I determined to pursue the course which had been recommended to me, but possibly by a somewhat more determined and less haphazard fashion than that which my French client would have followed. Though at this stage of my career I knew that I possessed a talent for making observations and for deducing the facts of a matter from details that would pass unremarked by many, in this case there was no evidence to present itself for my study. My task here was therefore to place myself in a position where such details would present themselves to my gaze.

"You may say, Watson, that so much of detective work is the piecing together of facts. Well, so it is, but it is the initial accumulation of those facts that is essential. I will not say that any fool can follow the threads once they are placed in his hands, but it is considerably easier to do this than it is to discover those threads in the first place.

" I accordingly presented myself at the rear entrance of the London house of Lord ___ who had served the brandy, in the guise of a representative of an importer of wines and spirits, and asked if I might speak to the butler of the house. Though in many houses, the choice of wine is that of the master of the house, in many others the butler takes on the task of

---

†   Note by Watson : I now know that Mr. Sherlock Holmes is no longer engaged in those activities on behalf of H.M. Government, and I feel that I am able to disclose the fact, as indeed I did in the adventure I entitled " His Last Bow".

deciding what the family is to drink.

"The housemaid accepted the card that I presented – I had taken the liberty of inventing a position and an employer for myself, but had decided to retain my own name, since at that point I was relatively unknown to the world – and carried it in while I cooled my heels on the mat. At length she returned, and informed me that the butler would be good enough to spare me ten minutes of his time.

"With an introduction such as that, I fully expected to encounter a pompous jack-in-office, and I was not disappointed. I had roughened my speech and my accents, and Gittins, for that was the name of the man, accordingly felt me to be his social inferior and treated me as such. It was obvious that he had granted me an audience merely so that he could have the pleasure of refusing my entreaties to buy wine from my pretended employer.

"However, despite his rudeness, I was able to discover the name of his current supplier, and this formed the next port of call on my journey."

"Were you not," I asked, "somewhat concerned lest he take you up on your offer and attempt to buy wine from you?"

"I flattered myself that I had sufficient mental resources to deal with that eventuality," Holmes smiled. "I had ensured that the prices I was giving him were well in excess of the market prices charged for the poor quality of wine that I was offering. In any event, the circumstance did not arise.

"I therefore made my way to the warehouse of the wine merchant whose name I had obtained. This was Vamberry, whose name, more than any other, I now associate with this case. Naturally, by now I had ceased to play the role of a representative of a wine merchant, and I presented myself as a foolish young rake-hell, well supplied with money from a deceased parent, who was determined to stock his cellar with the most expensive and impressive liquors that money could buy. This brought me, as I had anticipated, into the private office of Vamberry himself.

"The man in question was obviously a sampler of his own wares. Indeed, he did more than simply sample them, if his red nose and broken veins were anything to go by. Decanters of various spirits stood in a line behind his desk, and wine glasses were very much in evidence. It seemed to me that such trappings were a little unbusinesslike. Still, if a man's business is selling wine, then wine will inevitably find its way into his business premises, so perhaps I was a little harsh in my judgements there.

"As it happens, as you know, I am partial to a light hock, and I commenced my enquiries in this direction. At first he attempted to fob me off by singing the praises of a rather mediocre Moselle, but I was soon able to persuade him of my bona fides in that area, and we arranged that I would take delivery of a somewhat overpriced Rhine wine. I had no doubt that the expense I incurred would be recompensed by the French government when I presented my final reckoning to them.

"'But,' I said to Vamberry, and lowering my voice to what I hoped was a suitable confidential whisper, 'the reason I came to you and to no other dealer in these things is on account of a superb old cognac I enjoyed the other day at the house of Lord ___, which I was informed was supplied by your firm.' I proceeded to give the details of the cognac as I had been supplied them by Duclasse.

"He appeared to be a little taken aback by this, but rallied with an answer. 'The brandy in question, sir, was indeed a fine spirit. Supplies of such a liquor are, of course, limited, and I regret to inform you that we have no more of that particular vintage in stock. Maybe I can interest you in this

Armagnac,' he added, gesturing towards one of the decanters behind him. 'Allow me to offer you a sample, sir. You will find that it is not, of course, up to the standard of that which you enjoyed at your friend's house – I am sure you are well aware that nothing can approach that – but I think you will find this a satisfactory substitute.' So saying, he picked up one of the glasses and made as if to pour a little of the contents of the decanter into it, but I spoke.

"'Thank you, but no. I really must insist on knowing where you discovered this nectar of the gods that I enjoyed the other night,' I told him.

"He smiled. 'You may insist all you please, my dear sir, but I will not divulge my sources to you, I assure you of that. All that I can say is that a very limited quantity was discovered in France and sent here. Now all the bottles have been sold, and there is no more to be had, in this country at least. Should you desire to find some, I would suggest that you cross the Channel and search for yourself, but I fear your search will be a long and fruitless one.' He smiled, not altogether pleasantly. 'Now that I have informed you of this, sir, maybe I can tempt you with some of this Armagnac ? No ? A shame, sir, if I may say so. To where shall I have the hock delivered ?'

"I gave him my Montague-street address, and left the building, now convinced that Vamberry was well aware of the nefarious origins of the brandy. I made my way to the French embassy and paid a call on M. Duclasse, where I asked him for the name of the supplier of wines and spirits to the Élysée, without, however, telling him where I had just visited.

"'My dear M. Holmes,' he said to me, laughing. 'There are so many who compete for the honour. I could not even begin to give you a complete list.'

"'But who,' I insisted, 'was responsible for delivering the

brandy that was stolen? That is the only point at issue, is it not?'

"'Very well,' he said to me, consulting a paper which he extracted from a file. 'The name of the firm is Vanbeur et Fils.' By now I knew I was on the right track. The name of Vanbeur would easily become Vamberry once anglicised, and the coincidence was too strong for me to ignore. I requested and received the address of this Paris merchant, and left London for Paris a couple of hours later.

"It was a challenge for me to be working in a city with which I was not completely familiar. Although I possessed a good working knowledge of Paris, it was not the complete working knowledge of the streets and alleyways of London that I had almost completely developed at that time.

"I found lodgings in a small pension close to the Parc Monceau, from where it was easy for me to reach the area in Montmartre where the wine merchant's premises were located. Before I visited there, however, I sent a note to François Le Villard, a detective in the Parisian service, with whom I had a friendship. I believe that I once showed you a letter of his when you and I first became acquainted‡, in which he expounded his gratitude to me in overly fulsome Gallic terms."

"How did you first come to meet him?" I asked.

"I think I explained earlier that I had spent many summers of my youth in France," replied Sherlock Holmes. "Le Villard was the child of a neighbour, and even as boys we discovered a common love of solving the problems encountered in detective work. After he had joined the Paris police and I had gone up to University, we maintained our contact with each other. As you know, I have been able to do him a good

---

‡   Editor's note: This is recorded in the first chapter of *The Sign of the Four.*

turn once in a while, and the reverse also held true on occasion, such as now.

"We met in a small restaurant, not far from the firm of Vanbeur, and talked over old times. I enquired if by chance he knew Duclasse, the French representative in London. It was hardly a bow drawn at a venture – the detective branch of the Paris police is relatively small – and he was able to inform me that Duclasse was highly regarded and his words were not to be ignored.

"I then told him, in the strictest confidence, which I had no doubt at all that he would keep, about the mission with which I had been entrusted by Duclasse. He expressed some surprise that Duclasse had selected me, rather than the Paris police force, to carry out this task, but seemed ready enough to assist me where possible.

"My next question was regarding the ease of entry into the Élysée Palace, since I knew that my friend had spent some time as part of the guard there. I was informed that, in a system that is typical of Gallic bureaucracy, every worker at the Palace is furnished with a kind of passport, containing their name and physical description, and countersigned by the Prefect of Police. This paper must be shown every time the worker enters or leaves the Palace. For visitors other than members of the Cabinet, a similar document is prepared and must be shown, and their names are entered into a register which is countersigned when they leave the premises."

"Then much of your work was done for you," I exclaimed. "Since you knew that the brandy had been stolen within the previous six months, all the names were in front of you."

"My dear Watson," Holmes answered me, shaking his head, "you can have no idea how many people pass in and out of that building every day. It would have been the work of years to examine those registers and to eliminate those who were there on their lawful occasions. In any event, the registers would not be made available to me, even if I were to produce a written order from Duclasse himself. It was obvious that a little more of an indirect approach was called for.

"The next day, I stationed myself outside the door of Vanbeur's establishment, dressed in the fashion of a typical Parisian *flâneur*. Indeed, so successful was my disguise that it attracted the attention of the gendarmes, who asked me to move on and stop loitering. Naturally, I complied with these requests, and then returned a little later.

"As I watched the comings and goings, there was one young man in particular who attracted my attention. He was dressed elegantly, almost dandyish in his appearance, and strolled in and out of the building several times during the course of the morning, for no apparent purpose other than to drink a cup of coffee in a neighbouring café or to purchase cigarettes from the *tabac*. From the deference with which he was greeted by the porter every time he passed that worthy's position, I deduced that he must be the Fils of Vanbeur et Fils.

" On his fourth exit from the building that morning, he vanished around the corner of the street. My guess was that he was bound for a restaurant for his lunch, and I decided, since I too was feeling the pangs of hunger, that I would follow him there. Once around the corner, he took a cab, and I likewise hired one, instructing it to follow the other. To my astonishment, his cab drew up outside the Élysée Palace.

" I paid off my jarvey, and watched him as he stood outside the gates of the building, making no attempt to enter. After about five minutes, his patience (and mine) were rewarded, when a fashionably dressed young demoiselle came out of the gate, showing a paper to the guard on duty as she did so.

"From what I had been told by Le Villard, this signified that she was employed within the palace, since she did not need to countersign a register. French fashions and modes of dress and so on differ from those in England, and I was unable to place her profession exactly, but it seemed to me that she was more than a domestic servant, and probably held some sort of clerical position, possibly operating a typewriting machine.

"The man whom I had cast as the son of the enterprise greeted this young person with some signs of affection, and they strolled arm in arm along the street for some two hundred yards before disappearing into a small bistrot. It was difficult for me to judge from my position, but it seemed to me that her affection towards him was more strongly demonstrated than his towards her. I felt it inadvisable to enter the same restaurant that they had entered, but refreshed myself with a small glass of wine in the café opposite.

"As you probably are aware, the French enjoy extended meals, and it was a full ninety minutes before the couple emerged. I was happy to leave my position, and follow them back to the Élysée, walking this time, and watching them bid farewell to each other as she re-entered the building."

I chuckled. "I have little sympathy for you, and I think that most would agree with me. Few would pity your having to sit in a Parisian café, drinking wine."

"I agree with you that there might be a slightly idyllic construction placed on the circumstances, but I can assure you that there really is very little pleasurable about such an occupation," Holmes smiled. "But I now had a very definite chain of events mapped out in my mind. The English wine merchant who supplied the brandy to his Lordship was undoubtedly connected to the one in Paris who had supplied to the President's household. And quite apart from the professional connection, it seemed that there was also a personal link to the Presidential household, in the form of the young man and the young lady. However, I was as yet unsure as to what that link actually might be.

"It seemed that my best line of attack, if I may phrase it that way, would be to find out more about the girl. Accordingly I stationed myself outside the Palace that evening, waiting for her to come out of the building. The somewhat distinctive red shawl that I had remarked her as wearing earlier in the day made her easy to pick out from the crowd, and I soon found an opportunity to collide with her, and to knock her reticule to the ground.

"I apologised in English, which she appeared to understand, and added some comments in a broken French. I insisted strongly that she take a glass of wine or some such with me, as I was concerned for her health, and she, seemingly nothing loth, accepted my invitation.

"As I had hoped, I was able to obtain some more information about her. She did indeed operate a typewriter in the Palace, in the department of the commissary, responsible for the food and drink consumed in there. Not only did she work in that department, it seemed that a large part of her job was the keeping of the records of the cellar's contents. It seemed to me to be a somewhat unusual responsibility for a young girl, but then I remembered that I was in France, and things are done differently there."

"So now you had all the pieces of the puzzle?" I hazarded.

"Indeed. That is the way it seemed to me. Given her position, it would be possible for her to remove anything from the cellars and pass it to her lover without anyone's being the wiser. The link between Paris and London I had already established to my satisfaction, as I said. When I had made my farewells to Mlle. Grangier, the name of my new acquaintance, I walked back to my lodgings, pondering how I could best prove beyond all doubt that which I knew to be true. It is one thing to have suspicions bordering on certainty, and quite another to have proof that will stand as evidence in a court of law."

"It was necessary for me to set a trap, and for that I required the assistance of Duclasse in London and my friend Le Villard in Paris. It would, naturally, be against all the established rules for them to act as agents provocateurs, but as one who works outside the official organisations, it seemed to me to be perfectly in order for me to do so.

"First, I went to Le Villard, and asked him whether there was a cypher which could be used to send messages to Duclasse in London. Naturally, I explained, it was not my intention to use the cypher myself, but I would be grateful if Le Villard could act on my behalf in this matter. He was to keep the contents of the cypher I sent and any that might be received in reply a secret from his colleagues. He made me swear on my honour that I was not engaged in any activity contrary to the interests of the Republic, but once I had done this, he was the very soul of cooperation.

"By the by, I happened to catch sight of the methods of encypherment used by the police departments of France. It is of a delightful and somewhat unexpected simplicity, and I had great pleasure in presenting it to Mycroft as a souvenir of my sojourn across the Channel. I do not feel that I broke my oath to Le Villard by so doing.

"I requested Duclasse to furnish me with the details of a wine that was known to be in the Élysée cellars, and not otherwise obtainable, if such a thing existed. He was able to cable back the details of a claret which had been laid down some forty-five years earlier, and of which vintage a mere couple of dozen remained. All of these, to the best of his knowledge, were to be found in the cellars of the Élysée. I now had the bait for my trap, and the next day I made my way to Vanbeur et Fils, in my guise of an over-rich and somewhat gullible Englishman.

"I demanded, in bad French, to see the proprietor, and after a short while was shown into the sanctum of M. Vanbeur. The family resemblance to Vamberry in London was remarkable.

"Still using my deliberately poor French, which he interpolated with equally broken and accented English, we discussed the matter at hand. I told him that I had heard, in great confidence, that his company was a specialist in procuring rare vintages for connoisseurs. At this, he expressed great surprise, and assured me with what appeared to be the utmost sincerity that this was not the case at all. Even when I played my trump card, and mentioned the brandy at Lord ___'s, it seemed to produce no visible results, and his face showed no sign of recognition.

"'I am sorry to be unable to assist you,' he said at length, 'but whoever gave you that information was sadly misinformed. We are a respectable house here, with a fine selection of wines available, but we are not, and we never have pretended to be, a specialist in the kind of rare brandy that you describe, though it may be that we have handled such matters once or twice in the past on a basis of strict confidence as regards the seller and the purchaser. If you are truly interested in obtaining this kind of thing, I can give you the addresses of several merchants who claim to specialise in the supply of rare wines. I cannot of course,' and here he shrugged, 'guarantee that what they supply is the genuine article. There are many rogues in this business.'

"I thanked him, and accepted the list that he gave me. I left his office and made my way towards the entrance of the building, feeling that in this case I was mistaken and I had probably set myself on a wild goose chase. However, before I reached the door, I was intercepted by the young man whom I had seen earlier with the young woman working at the Palace. He caught at my sleeve and spoke to me in English, without a trace of a French accent.

"'I heard you speaking to my uncle just now,' he said to me in a low voice. 'I apologise if this may seem impertinent to you, but my office is next to that of my uncle, and I cannot help overhearing some of the things that pass in there. If you would do me the honour of taking a cup of coffee with me, or perhaps something a little stronger, in the café across the road, I believe I may be able to help you in your search.'

"As you may imagine, I heard this speech with some relief that my deductions so far appeared to be correct. I naturally accepted the invitation, but refused his proffered arm as we strolled to the nearest cafe and ordered our refreshments – coffee for me, and absinthe for my new friend.

"'My name is Vamberry,' he began. 'The gentleman you have just seen, the owner of the establishment, is my father's brother. My father, do you see, operates the same kind of business as his brother, in London rather than Paris. I am expected to succeed my father in the London business, and accordingly he has sent me to Paris to learn the trade at this end for a few years.'

"'And what sort of business do you yourself do?' I asked him.

"He looked at me sharply. 'I do not take your meaning,' he said to me.

"'I took the impression from your words just now that you were engaged in a somewhat different line to that of your uncle and your father,' I said. 'You say that you heard my conversation with your uncle?' He nodded. 'Then you are aware of my search for this wine, of which I have heard so much, and which appears to be unobtainable at any price.'

" He dropped his voice to a low volume, so that even I with my acute hearing had to strain to catch his words. 'The wine you are seeking is almost unobtainable,' he informed me. 'I happen to know, however, where it may be possible to lay hands on a dozen. But you are mistaken when you say that it is unobtainable at any price. There is indeed a price.'

" 'Name it,' I commanded him. He did so, and even though I had previously heard of the large sums of money commanded by such vintages, I was somewhat taken aback by the amount, and I fear that my surprise showed somewhat in my face. He noticed this, and laughed. 'More than you are prepared to pay?' His tone was mocking, and I must confess, Watson, that this irked me.

" 'I am well prepared, and well able, to afford such sums,' I told him stiffly. 'However, you should be aware that I am not in the habit of paying out such large amounts without having first seen and examined the merchandise for which I am paying.'

" His face fell a little at this, but he rallied. 'There may be some expenses involved in procuring the wine,' he informed me.

" 'Quite possibly there will be,' I said. 'Without wishing to know the details, I can guess that certain parties will have to be compensated for their activities.'

" He nodded in agreement. 'I am glad to see that you understand the situation.'

" 'If I am understanding the nature of your business correctly, though, this is not the first time that you have performed such service for a special customer. I would therefore expect you to have some money saved from such previous transactions, which you may use for these purposes. I must reiterate that under no circumstances will I pay money without having seen and thoroughly inspected the goods for myself. It is a matter of principle with me. If it will make you feel any happier, I will repay those expenses, provided always that I am furnished with a properly itemised statement of your outgoings. This would, of course, be in addition to the price that we have already agreed for the wine.'

"As I had imagined, his face brightened a little at this suggestion. 'Very well, then,' he agreed. 'You require a full dozen?' I told him that a half-dozen would be sufficient, at the price he was naming. 'I must warn you that it will take at least one week, possibly two, before I can make the delivery to you,' he said.

"'That is perfectly acceptable to me, and I am content to wait. You may contact me by leaving a message at my pension,' and I wrote the name and address of my lodgings on a blank card and handed it to him.

"'And your name?'

"I gave the name I was using at the pension, which happened to be the name of a University acquaintance of mine. I further informed him that I proposed to be absent from Paris for a week, and there would be little point in his attempting to contact me before my return. In actual fact, I had no intention of leaving the city, but proposed to use the time in observing this young man and his accomplice, or accomplices."

"You must have sorely missed your Baker-street Irregulars," I remarked. "I cannot imagine that now you would be content to spend several days in that fashion."

Holmes smiled. "You seem to forget, Watson, that I was them at the start of my career, and I had no organisation such as that available to me in London, let alone in Paris. It occurred to me that I could involve the police at this early stage, but despite my high opinion of their abilities,

especially when compared with those of the London police
at that time – I do not make comparisons with today's force,
which has improved considerably, and I may say, without appearing to be boasting, at least partly as a result of my efforts – I was concerned lest they act prematurely and prevent
the capture of those behind this scheme. I was convinced, do
you see, that the idea and the execution of these thefts and
subsequent resale was not the work of the young dandy who
now sat before me.

"As it happened, I was completely wrong in this last assumption. The somewhat foppish exterior of the young man
apparently concealed a criminal mind which, had it survived,
could possibly have equalled that of Professor James Mori-
arty in its capacity for mischief and villainy. But I am leap-
ing ahead of myself in the recounting of this story. The next
chapter, or act in this drama if you will, is, I suppose, of some
interest, though my part in it was almost entirely a passive
one.

"The next week that I passed in Paris was one of the most
physically demanding that I had ever spent in my life. I had
determined to see the whole business through on my own,
up until the final curtain, to revert to our theatrical meta-
phor. This meant keeping watch on the Vanbeur establishment, and particularly on the younger member of that family,
for anything up to fourteen hours in any one day. I was on
my feet in the street for the vast majority of that time, and it
was one of those wet springs for which Paris is infamous. I
had visited the old clothes market and provided myself with
a variety of outfits, and I could change my appearance with
the help of some theatrical make-up. I was reasonably certain that my constant vigils would repay the considerable discomfort in which I often found myself.

"In fact, it was on the second day after I had spoken to

young Vamberry that my patience was first rewarded. On the previous day he had met his young lady for their luncheon as usual, and the next day I was pleased to see that shape of a bottle was clearly visible in the bag she was carrying as she walked through the gates of the Palace. On her return back to work that afternoon the bag was obviously empty and his attaché case appeared to be heavier than when he had met Mlle. Grangier earlier. I had to assume that a bottle, as specified by young Vamberry to his accomplice the day before, had been transferred between them during their meal in the restaurant.

The next day and the next, the process was repeated, and I now felt it was time to acquaint Le Villard with my discoveries. He was highly intrigued by my account, and expressed his wish to move immediately against Vamberry and Grangier, but I persuaded him to wait for at least one day, and to set the trap with a number of officers waiting outside the Palace, dressed in plain clothes. The French certainly handled this sort of affair much better than our London police did in the past – though things have changed, as I say – and all was arranged as the couple met as usual at the gates of the Élysée Palace.

"The pair invariably took their meal at the same restaurant, and Le Villard had arranged things so that two of his officers were waiting inside for them. Two more, one of them a female police agent – again, the French were far in advance of us in these matters at that time – followed them inside the restaurant after a few minutes.

"Le Villard had arranged that when the bottle was handed over by Grangier to Vamberry, we would be summoned into the restaurant by the sound of a police whistle. It transpired that we did not have long to wait, and the anticipated blast came within a few minutes.

"Le Villard burst through the door into the restaurant, with myself close at his heels, where we beheld the guilty pair sitting, thunderstruck, and seemingly unable to believe what was happening to them. On the table was a bottle of the priceless claret about which I had been informed by Duclasse.

"'You!' shrieked the young woman, as she saw and recognised my face, and young Vamberry, following the direction of her pointing finger, likewise gave a start of recognition.

"'You are a police spy!' he spat out at me. 'You Judas! You treacherous worm!' and many more epithets, all of an equal amity, followed.

"Le Villard corrected him. 'This gentleman has no official connection with the police,' he informed Vamberry. 'He is merely an honest citizen doing his duty.'

"Any fight seemed to go out of Vamberry abruptly. He sat limply in his chair, a somewhat pathetic sight. As you know, Watson, I am a staunch believer in the virtues that have made our nation a great one, and it was a source of considerable embarrassment to me to watch an Englishman, guilty as he was, on the verge of weeping like a child. 'My father must never know of this,' he kept repeating.

"I was surprised by these words. I had imagined that the whole business was known to the older Vamberry, who had sold the purloined brandy to Lord ___. It appeared from his son's words that this was none of his doing. 'Tell me who is behind these thefts,' I commanded the young man, 'and I will do my best to make sure that things go easier for you. This villainy is more than just your doing, of that I am sure.'

"'You are mistaken, There is no-one,' he said. 'This is my idea, and mine alone. When I was sent to Paris by my father, it occurred to me that it might be possible for me to provide some special services for those who wanted something a little off the menu, as it were.' He smiled wanly. 'You are only the second such customer.'

" 'The first being Lord ____, I assume ? '

" ' Indeed, though he made the purchase through my father, who was completely unaware, I assure you, of the origins of this brandy. My father simply passed on the request, little knowing that I had placed myself in a position where I was actually able to fulfil it. I knew, do you understand, that my uncle was the merchant who had dealt with the original discoverer of the cases, and who had then sold them to the Palace. The whole business was kept very secret, but since I had access to my uncle's ledgers, I knew all.'

" 'And how was mademoiselle here unaware of what was going on ? ' asked Le Villard. 'Or did she share in the profits with you ? '

" 'I helped him for love,' replied the young girl defiantly. 'Not for money, but for love.' At this, the corners of the young man's mouth twitched, and he sniggered unpleasantly.

" 'Did you really believe I loved you ? ' he laughed at her. There was something wild and almost hysterical in the way he uttered these words.

" The girl turned to him, with a look of utter hatred in her eyes as she realised he was mocking her.

" 'Did you believe me ? ' he repeated. 'I had to find a way into the Palace cellars, and you were the easiest route. I had heard of you and of your duties at the Palace from a mutual friend, and I found an opportunity to meet you. Thank you for all your help.' He made a mocking half-bow in her direction.

" Her face convulsed with rage, and she snatched up one of the sharp knives on the table and lunged at him, plunging it into his chest. Immediately, Le Villard and his men seized her and pinioned her arms as she shrieked obscenities at her former supposed lover in a vile Parisian dialect that I could barely comprehend. Meanwhile, two of the other agents seized Vamberry, one of them clapping a napkin to the wound to staunch the flow of blood."

"It sounds like a terrible scene," I said. "I remember seeing nothing of this anywhere in the newspapers or anywhere. I would have imagined that such a sensational event would have been reported to the public."

"The French police seem to control the press in a much stronger fashion than we do ours," Holmes told me. "The waiters and the other customers in the restaurant were immediately sworn to secrecy, under severe penalties, by the agents there. Vamberry and his accomplice were taken out of the back door of the restaurant, and taken away ; the girl to the cells, and Vamberry to the hospital.

"I never saw Vamberry again. Despite the efforts of the surgeons, he perished from loss of blood that very night. In my opinion, he had no great will to continue living. Despite his mocking manner towards the girl and his callousness in that regard, there did seem to be a genuine sense of shame when he talked about his father, and it could well be that he had no wish to face an angry parent. In any event, an examination of his accounts after his death revealed that he was deeply in debt as the result of his losses at cards. It was undoubtedly this that had led him to the desperate measures that he had adopted."

"And the girl ? "

"I saw her once after that fatal incident – at her trial for murder. I was called as a witness. She was found guilty and died by the guillotine." Holmes recounted these facts in a flat voice, devoid of any emotion or feeling.

"And the theft of the brandy and the wine ? "

"That was never mentioned in court. The trial was held

in camera, and in any event, she did not offer any circumstances relating to the events in her defence. I confess that I felt not a little pity for her. She had obviously been flattered by the extravagant attentions that had been paid to her by young Vamberry who had been introduced to her by a mutual friend, as he had said. But it was not my place to plead on her behalf, and in any event, she had betrayed the trust that had been placed in her for her work in the Palace."

"And the father? Vamberry the elder?"

"He was informed by Duclasse in London that his son had died in a street brawl with Apaches. His son had told us, and Duclasse skilfully and discreetly established it as a fact, that he had no knowledge of his son's activities. He died last week, as I read in the *Times*, his brother Vanbeur having passed away some time soon after the incidents I describe. I was reluctant to recall the story to you while he was still alive."

"What was the fate of the wine and brandy?"

Holmes chuckled. "Thereby hangs a little tale. The brandy which had been sold to Lord ___ remained in his cellars. Duclasse felt it would be impossible to retrieve it from there without a long and embarrassing explanation. As it happens, I had the privilege of tasting some of that brandy when I was entertained by Lord ___ some time afterwards. I had been engaged by him on a matter of some delicacy, which you have recorded in your accounts of our adventures, Watson, and I was invited to dine with him to explain the facts of that case.

"The brandy, by the way, was everything that had been claimed for it. This brandy here," and he indicated the bottle in front of us, "is certainly a fine one, but it cannot hold a candle to the memory of that glass poured for me by Lord ___ himself."

"And the wine?"

"That is where the tale hangs. The three bottles that had previously been removed and secreted in Vamberry's lodgings were removed and returned quietly to the Palace."

"But there was a bottle on the table in the restaurant," I said. "What happened to that?"

"That is the tale. Strange to tell, that bottle was never seen again. At least it was never seen by anyone save Le Villard and myself. Somehow, the bottle found its way into Le Villard's capacious coat pocket, and from there, some time later the same evening, onto a table that stood between him and me."

"And..?" I asked, amused by this confession.

"It was too thin, and there were overtones of tannin there which were not to my taste. It was, however, perfectly drinkable, though hardly worth a fraction of what I had been asked to pay for it by young Vamberry." He paused and sipped at his brandy. "In any event, Watson, the full measure of a fine drink is only achieved when it is shared between true friends. Do you not agree?"

"Most heartily," I answered, and raised my own glass to him in reply.

The Singular Affair of the Aluminium Crutch

"I HAD JUST CLOSED UP MY SHOP, AND I WAS
WALKING TOWARDS MY HOME NEARBY, WHEN
ALMOST THE SAME THING HAPPENED AGAIN. THIS
TIME, IT WAS THREE MEN, RATHER THAN TWO."

EDITOR'S NOTES

As always, the dispatch-box continues to intrigue and to mystify.

In "The Musgrave Ritual", as mentioned earlier in this volume, Sherlock Holmes shows Watson a large tin box containing a number of mysteries, "a third full of bundles of paper tied up with red tape into separate packages".

"These were all done prematurely ; before my biographer came along to glorify me," he explains to Watson, and proceeds to give a list, well known to those who study the life and work of Sherlock Holmes. Among these, a few have excited interest, partly on account of Holmes' rather fanciful description of them that he provided to Watson, and one of these is "the singular affair of the aluminium crutch".

So, when I came across a bundle of paper in the envelope marked "Before My Time", done up with red tape, and entitled "Alum. Crutch" in the handwriting that I have learned to recognise as that of Sherlock Holmes, you may imagine my excitement. Here was the case that even Watson was not allowed to see, presented for my interest and inspection.

When I opened the papers, though, I discovered that John Watson had been ahead of me. Though the case was undoubtedly and unmistakably the one referred to by Sherlock Holmes, and contained a sheet of the original brief notes in the detective's writing, it was clear that Watson had conversed with Holmes on this subject, and had expanded the notes, though leaving the story as one told by Holmes. As always, we cannot assume the dialogue as reported by Watson to be a faithful representation of the actual words spoken at the time, or even the words as reported by Holmes.

It must be admitted that the narrative is much diminished by the absence of John Watson. He has faithfully recorded some *of Holmes' introspections, as presumably recounted to him, but the voice of common-sense seems to be missing, as is the more human touch he brings to the adventures of his famous friend.*

The case, such as it is, does not provide Holmes with much opportunity to display his powers of deduction or observation, but as he himself remarks, these were not necessarily as developed as they were later in his career. It remains, nonetheless, as an interesting addition to the chronicles of Sherlock Holmes.

HOLMES' ACCOUNT OF THE CASE (AS WRITTEN BY DR. WATSON)

THE case of which I am writing occurred before my remove to Baker-street. I was setting up my practice and establishing my credentials as a practitioner of the science of detection, but cases were few and far between at the start of my career, and I welcomed almost any client with open arms.

Such a client was Mr. Timothy Gosling, who presented himself at my door one morning. My rooms were on the fourth floor of the house where I had taken lodgings in Montague-street. I fear that Mr. Gosling had found it to be a sore trial to mount the stairs up to the room, given that his right leg was missing below the knee, and he was forced to make his way using a crutch. He was breathing more heavily than I would have expected, even given the physical exertion he had just undertaken, and I made a mental diagnosis of an asthmatic condition.

He gave me his name, and I invited him to sit in the chair that I reserved for the use of my clients, facing the window, in a position where the light fell full upon them, enabling me to take note of their faces, while I sat with my back to the window, which effectively masked my expressions and moods from their eyes.

Upon my demanding the nature of his business, he answered me in a voice which seemed surprisingly cultured for a man of his somewhat rough appearance. I had previously marked him as a former sailor — his tattoos and the way in which he automatically ducked his head to avoid the door lintel as he crossed the threshold had informed me of that fact — and he informed me that he had served on H.M.S.

Cossack in the Baltic in the course of the Crimean War, where he had lost his leg to a Russian shell.

"But it's this crutch I have here that's causing me problems, if you see, sir," he told me.

I examined the instrument in question from a distance, but could perceive nothing out of the ordinary, other than it appeared to be made of some dull metal. He noticed the direction of my gaze, and added, "No there's nothing the matter with it, sir. Nothing that strange about it that I can tell, except it's made of metal, as you can see. And that's the problem."

"What do you mean?" I asked. "Why are you here?"

"Ah, this crutch is the nub of the matter, Mr. Holmes. I have experienced a most curious event twice in the last few days, and I have reason to believe that it is all on account of this here crutch of mine."

"That promises to be a little more interesting than what you have told me about your past," I said to him. "Pray, tell me more."

"Well, sir, first I should perhaps tell you how I came about using this crutch," he said. "After I lost my leg, I was first sent to the Royal Hospital at Haslar. They took good care of me, and I was lucky enough to survive when so many of the poor b___s, if you'll pardon the language, sir, didn't. They offered me a peg-leg, but I didn't want one of those. I saw the trouble the others have with them, and so I decided to ship out without the extra spar fitted, as you might say. I left the Hospital with the ordinary kind of wooden crutch, and that served me well.

"Before I had joined the Andrew, I had received some training as a cobbler, and that was the trade I took up once more." I had already noted the wear on the trousers, and the strange deformation of the thumb that I believed to be characteristic of that occupation, but at that stage in my career it was beneficial to have such observations confirmed, and I was not about to lose what little reputation I had in stating my guesses out loud, however well informed they might be. "Without wishing to boast about it, sir, I am good at what I do, and my little business of repairing boots and shoes soon attracted some wealthy customers who were glad to avail themselves of my services. One of these was the owner of a metal works, a Mr. Habgood, who interested himself in my condition, and was always ready to stop and talk.

"One day he visited me with a pair of boots to be mended, and asked me outright, 'How do you like that thing?' pointing to my crutch.

"I answered him that I found it heavy at times, and in wet weather, it was difficult to dry out.

"'If I were to make you a present of a crutch, constructed of a new metal, would you be willing to use it, and to let me have a report on how it feels to you?' he asked me. 'My company thinks that this will be of great interest to people in your condition, and none of the difficulties and problems you are currently experiencing with the wooden crutch would be present with this new model.'

"I answered him that surely a metal crutch would be heavy and cumbersome, and furthermore would be subject to rust. He laughed, and told me that the crutch would be constructed of a new metal, called 'aluminium', which would not rust, and was many times lighter than iron or steel. I have always had a mind that has enjoyed new things and new ideas, and I agreed to his suggestion.

"The next week he arrived to collect his boots, carrying the crutch you see before you now. You can see that it can be adjusted easily by means of these screws, and he most kindly fitted it up so that it was comfortable for me to use. From the first, the light weight made it easy for me to carry with me, and to get about with, and the fact that it could be dried so easily in wet weather also made it attractive for me, and I informed Mr. Habgood of this fact.

"'Excellent,' said he. 'When I come to collect the boots next week, you may tell me how you are getting along with it. I have high hopes for this design, and hope that soon all people in your unfortunate position may be able to use such a thing.

"Well, Mr. Holmes, sir, it may sound strange to you to hear a cripple such as myself singing the praises of such a simple thing as a crutch, but believe me, unless you have experienced such a thing for yourself, you cannot begin to conceive how pleasant it is to have such a thing to help you along your way.

"Be that as it may, I was able to suggest to Mr. Habgood some minor modifications and improvements to the original design and he was gracious enough to listen to my suggestions, taking the crutch away for half a day or so, in order to have the changes made at the works, before returning the improved crutch to me.

"About two weeks ago, I was just about to shut up my little shop in Wembley, and return home, when I was visited by two men. They told me that they had seen me with the new aluminium crutch, and asked me if I would sell it to them."

"Did they offer a good price?" I asked, smiling.

"They offered a price which was much higher than I would have thought possible," he answered me in all seriousness. "They proposed to pay me the sum of twenty pounds."

"That is indeed a considerable amount of money. But it appears that you refused the offer?"

"I did indeed, sir. I told them that the crutch, strictly speaking, was not mine to sell, and had been loaned to me by Mr. Habgood as the only one of its kind. It is quite possible that l was mistaken in that, but I really wished to keep it."

"And their reaction ? "

"They asked if they might examine the crutch. I handed it to them, and they appeared to be familiar with the way it had been assembled."

"How do you mean ? "

"As you can see here, sir," and here my visitor demonstrated, "you can remove the end of the crutch by unscrewing it. It is not obvious that this is possible, but it seemed that my attacker knew about it. He removed the end, and then he looked inside the tube of the crutch, as if he was looking for something, and held the crutch up in the air, and waved it about, as if he was trying to shake something out of it. Nothing came out, and he then turned his attention to the other end, which he removed. Again, it seemed to me that he knew exactly where to find the parts of the crutch that held it together. Once more he looked for some object inside the crutch, but he couldn't find anything.

"'Where is it ? ' he asked me, turning to me, with a terrible expression on his face. Well, of course, I had no idea of what he meant by this, and told him so. ' I'll fix you, you lying _____," he swore at me.

"I was saved from his wrath by his companion, who pointed out that there was no need to use any sort of violence towards me. The other seemed to agree with that, which was a relief to me, sir, I can tell you, and they left me in my shop, and my crutch in three pieces on the counter."

"One moment," I interrupted. "Would you know these men again if you saw them ? "

"I might be able to recognise them, sir, if I saw them again. It was getting dark, however, and I had not at that time lit the lamps. One thing I noticed, though was that I felt that they were not English, though they seemed to speak English well enough. Maybe Swedish or Danish or something like that. You see a lot in the Andrew, and you learn to notice these things. We were in the Baltic with the *Cossack*, and I picked up a little of those languages. There was one other thing. At one point, one of them said something like 'We were told it was in the crutch'."

"That may well prove to be of importance," I told him. "But they found nothing, and they took nothing from you?"

"Nothing," he confirmed. "They did not seem to have any interest in me at all, just in the crutch."

"I take it that you then went to the police?"

"I did not. After all, although one of them had expressed some anger, there was no real threat, let alone an act of violence."

"And since then?"

"A similar thing happened last night. I had just closed up my shop, and I was walking towards my home nearby, when almost the same thing happened again. This time, it was three men, rather than two."

"The same as on the previous occasion?" I asked.

My client shook his head. "I am almost sure that they were a different lot from those who had come round the time before," he told me. "Although it was hard for me to see their faces, the voices were different. They were still from that same part of the world, though, sir, as far as I could tell."

"Again, they wanted to buy the crutch off you?"

"That they did. This time, they offered thirty pounds, and a new wooden crutch. They were polite enough about asking me, but when I refused to sell it to them, they turned nasty on me. One of them started swearing at me in one of those languages—"

" Which language ? "

" One of those from up there in the Baltic, sir. Swedish or Danish, but I couldn't swear to which it was. They started to crowd in on me, and I was frightened about what was going to happen to me, I can tell you, when a bobby came around the corner, and they left pretty quick. The constable asked me what was going on, and I told him.

" Well, he was good enough to listen to me, and I was a bit shaken up, I can tell you that, sir. He suggested that I come along to the police station with him, where he would give me a cup of tea and let me tell my story.

" When I had told the sergeant on duty there of my little adventure, he suggested that I should take the crutch to pieces, so that he could look at it and see what was special about it. I did, but he could not see anything strange or remarkable.

" As I just told you, I was unable to give any description of the men, and although the police officers at the station told me that they were very sorry, they also said to me that there was nothing that they could do to provide any practical help in catching the men who had threatened me."

" That is so often the way with the official police," I remarked.

" But, sir, they have promised to station a constable outside my shop at the time when I close."

" That is something, I suppose," I admitted. " And now you are here ? "

" Yes. There is a Sergeant Morton at the station, who suggested that I come here.* He had heard of your name, and felt that you might be able to help me."

" I am in no position to offer you protection, such as the

---

*   This may well be the police officer, later promoted, and referred to as " Inspector Morton" in " The Dying Detective".

police are doing," I informed him.

"No, sir, that is not what I want. I want to know what is
the meaning of these visits, and what is the meaning of this
crutch, and why it seems to be so important."

"That may take some time, and also..." I have to confess
that at this stage in my career, I considered myself to be still
learning my trade, and I was not confident in the matter of
demanding fees from my clients. Happily, Mr. Gosling took
my meaning without my having to provide the embarrassing
details of fees and expenses.

"There's no need to be worried about money, sir. Before
I came here, I took the liberty of calling on Mr. Habgood,
and explaining what had happened. He was shocked and dis-
tressed that his gift to me should have had such results, and
he promised to make good any expenses that I might incur in
this business."

This, as you can imagine, relieved my mind somewhat. Though I was hesitant to ask for fees, I was nonetheless in need of money to pay for the necessities of life, not
to mention the materials I required in order to ply my trade
effectively.

At this date, by the way, there was no doubt in my mind
but that I was pursuing a trade – one of applied science, perhaps – but a trade nonetheless, until such time, that was, until I could raise it to the dignity of a profession.

I requested my new client to hand over the crutch for my
examination. As he had told me, it was indeed of a very light
weight, but at the same time of a sturdy construction. It certainly seemed to me that if the process of extracting the metal from the ore could be made cheaper, there would be a
future demand for this metal which could far exceed that for
steel.

However, such speculative thoughts were not conducive

to solving the problem now laid before me, and I examined the crutch, attempting to work out how it could be disassembled. Gosling offered to tell me the details, but I refused, preferring to discover the method myself.

After a minute's inspection, it proved a relatively simple process to remove the tip and to take apart the other end, and I examined the joints, and all relevant parts of the crutch, using a powerful lens. The whole appeared to be extremely well constructed, and machined with precision.

"This is an extremely well-made piece of work," I remarked to Gosling.

"It is indeed, sir," he agreed. "As a craftsman myself in another field, I have to agree with you there."

"Do you know what other business or objects Mr. Hapgood conducts and manufactures at his works?"

"No, sir. All I know is that it is a metal works."

"And the name of the company?"

He felt in his pocket, and produced a piece of paper, on which was written the name of Mr. James Habgood, and printed at the top was the name and address of his company, the Wembley Empire Metallurgic Works, Ltd. I withdrew my notebook from my pocket, and stood up to retrieve my pen from the desk by the window behind me. As I did so, I noticed two men standing idly on the pavement on the opposite side of the road to the house. They appeared to be waiting for something or somebody, and I called my visitor's attention to them, handing him the crutch to assist him to make his way to the window, while bidding him to keep out of sight of those below, as far as possible.

"Do you know those two?" I asked him.

"I cannot swear to it, but I would say that they are two of the ones who came to visit me last night, sir," he told me. "Yes, that's right," as one of them turned away. "There was a certain trick to his walk which I seem to recognise from the time before."

"I would say that it would be unwise for you to leave the house alone, at least carrying this crutch," I remarked. "That is to say, if the crutch really is the object of these unwelcome attentions, which would seem to be the case."

"What shall I do ?" he asked.

"It is simple," I told him. "I will ensure that you have a simple wooden crutch to support you while I make my enquiries, and I will let you out of the back door to the house, where you will not be seen." I stepped to the casement, taking care to hide myself from the two watchers below, and blew two short blasts and a long one on my police-whistle. The two men below looked up sharply at the noise, but were unable to distinguish anything as I dodged back behind the curtains.

After some five minutes, there was a knock at the door, and I admitted a street Arab who went by the name of Wiggins. I had employed the lad, and a number of his friends, on a few occasions in the past, and I had found his services to be well worth the minimal amount I paid for them.

"How much," I asked of my visitor, "would you expect to pay for a well-made wooden crutch ?"

"Somewhere in the region of four shillings, sir," he told me.

"Very well. Wiggins, here are five shillings. You are go to the hospital and procure a crutch for this gentleman here – of the best quality, mark you – and you may keep whatever remains of the five shillings. I advise you to depart and return by the back entrance."

Wiggins touched his forelock and departed on his errand. When he had departed, I ascertained more details regarding my client, but was unable to discover anything that would seem to have a bearing on the attacks on his person.

In a matter of twenty minutes, Wiggins returned, bearing a wooden crutch of an obviously high standard. "They told me that the person who this belonged to had no further use for it, and so I could have it cheap at three shillings," he announced proudly.

"In which case, I shall ask you to earn the extra money by assisting Mr. Gosling down the stairs, and out of the back door to the nearest Underground railway station. If anyone approaches you, you are to use whatever means you think necessary to see them off. You can do that?"

Wiggins assented, and I turned to Gosling. "This crutch will have to serve you until I return your aluminium crutch," I told him. "I trust it will be satisfactory."

"Entirely so," he told me. "If I had not had the aluminium crutch presented to me, this would be just what I would choose for myself."

With that, and my promise that I would let him know as soon as I discovered anything of interest, he and Wiggins left the room. I watched the two men opposite, who continued their watch for about two hours more, before finally appearing to lose interest and leave.

Naturally, I could not be sure whether they had lost interest, and I therefore placed the crutch in a prominent position before I left the room, on the assumption that if they were seeking the object, which appeared to be of no value or interest in my eyes, it was better that they came across it immediately, and did not feel it necessary to ransack the room in their search for it.

In any event, I felt it necessary not to waste time, and as soon as I had taken my luncheon, I made my way to the Enfield Empire Works managed by Mr. Habgood. These proved to be not so much a large manufactory, as a cluster of small brick buildings, from some of which issued smoke and fumes of a familiar chemical nature.

On presenting my card, I was admitted to the office of Mr. James Habgood, who received me with a little suspicion. He was a small man, with intense blue eyes that peered at me through thick spectacles. I was not prepared for the owner of the company to be dressed in a white laboratory coat, but he explained that he was not only the manager of the company, but its chief researcher.

Following Watson's chronicling of my little adventures, some fame has come my way, and the science of detection is a relatively familiar subject to those who read newspapers and magazines. At this stage of my life, though, it was necessary for me to introduce myself to Habgood, and explain exactly how I made my living, and to persuade him that any money he was to spend in my direction on behalf of the unfortunate cobbler would be money well spent.

After he had heard me out, he appeared to be sincerely interested in my way of life, and asked several questions which betrayed a keen intelligence.

" I had no idea that there were people such as yourself plying this trade," he said to me at one point.

" I am, as far as I am aware, the first, and to the best of my knowledge, the only consulting detective in London," I told him.

" Well, you may be just the person I am looking for, in that case," he told me. " Maybe I can tell you a little of our business, since you have been good enough to tell me something of yours, and you may decide whether you wish to pursue an enquiry of mine concurrently with that of poor Gosling. I had no idea when I presented him with the crutch that it could cause such a problem, but I sense that his problem may also be mine."

" Pray tell me," I invited him, "and I will decide whether to take your case or not."

"You are certainly a curious fellow," he said to me with a smile. "In any case, to begin. You have noted the name of this works ? " I nodded, and he continued. "We are not your usual metalworking factory, you understand. We develop new alloys and metalworking techniques all the time, which we then make available – at a price, of course – to companies engaged in the actual business of manufacturing."

"And aluminium is one of the materials with which you work, I take it ? Such as the crutch that you presented to Gosling ? "

Habgood chuckled. "You describe yourself as a professional man. I take it that you may therefore keep a secret in a professional manner ? " Naturally, I assented. "Do not worry, Mr. Holmes. I am not asking for a lifelong undertaking to keep your lips sealed. Merely for the next six months at the most. The crutch that I have loaned to Gosling contains one of our most valuable pieces of research."

" I examined the crutch closely," I told him, "and could see nothing contained in it."

He laughed in my face. " My dear sir," he said to me, " I am not in any doubt as to your ability to see what is in front of your eyes, or even to make deductions, such as you describe, from those observations. What is contained in Mr. Gosling's crutch is invisible to the eye. It is the material of which it is composed that is of interest."

"Aluminium, he told me."

"Ah, but it is not merely aluminium. There are other metals added, and a special process employed, that make the metal of a vital part of that crutch many times stronger than aluminium, and only a fraction heavier. Why, it could even be used as lightweight armour-plating against bullets, we believe."

"I am to take it that this recipe and this process are secret?"

"Indeed they are. The exact composition of this alloy and the method for its manufacture are known in their entirety to one person alone – myself. The details are kept in a safe in a bank. The only sample of the metal exists as a part of the crutch I have loaned to Gosling."

"Is it possible," I asked him, "to discover the elements composing the alloy and the process by which it has been made, through an examination of the material itself?"

"I believe that it is in theory possible, using the technique of spectroscopy. A trained metallurgist could deduce certain key processes by examining the substance through a high-powered microscope." I must have appeared a little crestfallen, because he added, "It is no reflection on you, Mr. Holmes, unless you consider yourself a metallurgist, that you were unable to identify the material. In any event, only a small part of the crutch is made of the durable aluminium alloy I have described."

"I am to assume that the Scandinavians attempting to purchase the crutch are in some way your business rivals?"

"That is correct," he told me. "The Swedes would give a lot to get their hands on the secrets of this alloy."

There was still something about his story which perplexed me. "Why have you used this alloy to make a crutch which you have given to a near-stranger?" I demanded. "Surely the sample would be best kept with the formula?"

"Ah, let me answer your questions," he said. "We had a very limited amount of this new alloy available to us, and we had no wish to increase the quantity until it had been tested outside our laboratories for durability, and resistance to the effects of the weather. A walking stick or some such would seem an ideal testing ground. But Gosling, to whom I have entrusted the repair of my boots and shoes for some time now, was in need of a crutch, and I therefore fashioned the object myself, incorporating the alloy at a critical point in its manufacture. I had always found Gosling to be completely honest and trustworthy, so I had no hesitation in providing him with the crutch, knowing that it would be in good hands."

"I am guessing that if I were to identify and dissuade your Swedish competitors from stealing your secrets, I would at once and the same time solve your problem, and that of Gosling."

"Indeed, Mr. Holmes. You have hit the nail on the head there."

"How do you think that the Swedes have discovered the alloy and its connection to Gosling?"

"There is no guesswork involved here, Mr. Holmes," he sighed. "My assistant in the development of the alloy was a very capable young man from Sweden who had worked with me for a number of years. Only two months ago, he suddenly left my employ, and I heard that he had returned to his native country, ostensibly to take care of his aged mother. Though in his time here I never showed him the precise formula for the alloy, or the secret of its preparation, I am sure that he gained nearly enough knowledge from the notes in my laboratory to be able to re-create the metal for himself. Svensson was a most talented young assistant," he sighed.

"But you feel that he has not the knowledge to make the alloy himself without a sample of the genuine article with which to compare it?"

"I would imagine that to be the case."

"And how would he come to know of its incorporation into the crutch?"

Habgood sighed once more. "While I was constructing the

crutch, I may have been careless in letting some of the piec-es, not including the part composed of the alloy, of course, remain overnight on the workbench. Svensson almost cer-tainly worked out what I was making."

"And the link to Gosling?"

"He knew of the fact that I used Gosling's services. In-deed, he too employed Gosling to repair his own shoes."

"And therefore was aware of Gosling's disability, and your compassion for the man?"

"I can only assume that to be the case."

"Then let us proceed on that assumption. I am willing to investigate this case, but I must advise you that I possess no official powers of arrest. Indeed, it is unlikely that any crime has been committed, from what I hear."

"The theft of my work is no crime?" he retorted.

"It would be necessary to prove that such a theft actually took place," I replied, "and that could be impossible to prove in a court of law, however much you and I are convinced of the thief's guilt."

"Very well. I would like you, then, to warn Svensson, or whoever it proves to be, that his attentions are not wel-come. If the company for whom he is currently working wish-es to obtain the secret of this alloy, it is not for sale to them."

"I will do my best," I told him.

He then proceeded to extend an invitation to me to tour the "works", which I accepted. The premises were in truth more of a laboratory than a manufactory, and which were of considerable interest to me from the point of view of chemistry.

"Well, Mr. Holmes," said to me as I concluded my visit, "it has been a pleasure to make your acquaintance, and I trust that you will be able to settle this matter to our satisfaction."

"And to that of Gosling, of course."

"Of course," he answered, shaking my hand in farewell.

As I returned to London, I was forced to consider a number of possible methods by which I could solve this problem. As I had told Habgood, there were no measures open to me by which I could invoke the rule of law to stop the Swedes from acquiring the crutch and thereby the knowledge of the alloy, which, from what I had been told, appeared to be of value to our country.

On approaching my lodgings in Montague-street, I noticed a dim light through the window of one of the rooms I occupied, warning me that I had an uninvited visitor. As usual, I was unarmed, other than for a swordstick which I had purchased on a whim in my University days, and which I carried with me. I let myself into the house as silently as was possible, and crept up the stairs.

Drawing my swordstick, and holding it in the approved *en garde* position that I had learned from my time spent with the foils, I quietly turned the handle of the unlocked door, and sprang into the room.

I beheld two tall fair-haired men bent over the table, on which lay the crutch, now disassembled. They looked up with a start and stood still when they saw the blade in my hand.

"We mean no harm," one of them said to me, in a voice which was recognisable as being un-English.

"We want to buy this," said the other, pointing to the crutch. "Fifty pounds."

"It is not mine to sell to you," I told them, firmly. "For any amount of money."

"Then we are sorry to have disturbed you," the first speaker said. They moved as if to leave the room, but I blocked the door, with the sword's tip pointing directly at the throat of the leader.

"You are staying here," I told them, and fixing my gaze on

them, pulled out my police whistle. "Two blasts on this, and my constables will come running. And you, my friends, will find yourself in prison on a charge of housebreaking."

At this, they appeared to be properly startled and dismayed. "There is, however," I told them, "a satisfactory solution which does not involve my officers. If you give me your word that you will leave this room, this city, and this country, and do not return, and you and your colleagues will make no further attempt to take or obtain what is not yours, then you may depart in peace."

The two looked at each other, and shrugged as one. "Very well. I have heard things about your English prisons, and I do not want to experience them."

I demanded their identities, which they furnished in the form of cards, whose contents I committed to memory. "Now go," I told them. Obediently, they left me, and I was pleased that my little deception of passing myself off as a police officer had been so successful.

The next day, I made a report to Habgood, taking the crutch with me, and he and I together returned the crutch to Gosling, assuring him that there would be no further attempts made to procure it. Habgood was as good as his word when it came to compensating me for the work I had carried out on Gosling's behalf, as well as for the service I had rendered him, and was kind enough to allow me to use his chemical laboratories from time to time when my own resources proved insufficient.

And that is the story of the aluminium crutch. The alloy, by the way, proved too expensive to manufacture in the quantity required for armour plating naval vessels, however. Habgood nonetheless believes that a use will be found for limited quantities of a strong lightweight alloy in specialised applications, but that day is not yet upon us.

❈

HOLMES' NOTES (ATTACHED TO WATSON'S ACCOUNT)

19 April, 1879 (Sat.)

Client : Timothy Gosling, cobbler, ex-sailor. Asthmatic. One leg (claims he lost the other in Crimean War).

Explained that he had been asked on two occasions to sell to foreigners (he claimed he identified them as Scandinavians) the unique aluminium crutch that he had acquired as a gift from an industrialist, but had refused to sell. Examined the crutch, but could see nothing unusual about it, other than the aluminium from which it had been constructed, being a somewhat unusual material to use for such an object, and the fact that it was an extraordinarily well-made piece of work.

Visited maker of the crutch (Habgood), to discover material forming crutch was unique new alloy, w/ many potential uses. Informed that Swede (ex-employee) had interest in this. Retained by maker to look into this matter.

Returned home to find two Swedes in my room examining crutch. Persuaded them to leave with threat of arrest and prosecution for housebreaking.

Recv'd from Habgood : £40 on his account and £5 on that of Gosling. Case closed.

The Case of the Abominable Wife

"EVEN THE CLOSED DOOR WAS NOT SUFFICIENT TO MASK THE SCREECHES AND SHOUTS, OFTEN ACCOMPANIED BY THE SOUNDS OF CRASHES AND BREAKING CROCKERY."

EDITOR'S NOTES

A story of Holmes without Watson, but told by Watson in his own style, though Holmes is nominally the narrator. By no means Holmes' most complex case, but one which sheds a little light on the human being behind the mask of the Great Detective. Mentioned in "The Musgrave Ritual" as one of the cases in Holmes' own tin box, which apparently contained a "...full account of Ricoletti of the club foot and his abominable wife".

 N the years of my association with Sherlock Holmes, I was well aware that there were many adventures which had occurred before my first meeting with him. He often provided hints as to their details, but was often reluctant to discuss them with me, providing merely tantalising glimpses of the past.

I have described some of them, based on his reminiscences, and frequently attempted to draw him out, as the phrase has it, regarding the others. However, it was difficult to find Sherlock Holmes in a state of mind that was conducive to extended conversation.

There was, however, one occasion when Holmes was constrained to idleness by the circumstances. We were crossing from Newhaven to Dieppe for a short holiday, and the boat was remarkably devoid of passengers, and hence of objects of interest for Holmes.

There was one passenger, however, who caught our eye as he limped along the deck. I recognised the signs of a club-foot, which obviously afflicted the poor fellow sorely.

" Did I ever tell you," asked Holmes, addressing me, " of the circumstances surrounding the club-footed Ricoletti and his abominable wife?"

" I recall you mentioning it at the time when you told me of the case involving your college friend Musgrave, but you provided no details."

"Then allow me to put this period of enforced idleness to some use and give you the full story. It is an interesting one, I think, though my methods at that time were somewhat crude and unrefined as compared to those I now employ. Although it is all written in full and reposes in that tin box in Baker-street, maybe you will permit me to indulge such narrative gifts as I possess and recount the tale to you as we make our way over to *la belle France.*

"I was working at the time of this case, as I think you know, from rooms in Montague-street. The good Mrs. Hudson had yet to enter my life, and you were unknown to me. I was slowly and painstakingly building up some sort of reputation among the professionals of Scotland Yard, chiefly Hopkins and Lestrade, and had come into contact with Gregson on a few occasions. However, the majority of my work, such as it was, during this period was relatively undemanding, and I found myself with more time on my hands than was desirable.

"I had not the resources to buy books with which to entertain myself, and the British Museum Reading Room was not wholly agreeable to me, given that smoking was prohibited there, and the limit on the number of books that might be consulted at one time I found irksome. As you know, when reading, one often finds oneself drawn to another related volume, following a skein of thought that may appear to be frivolous or illogical at first, but later proves to make perfect sense. The Museum's rules made it impossible for me to conduct research in the way I would have liked.

"It was also at this time, I confess, that I discovered some of the joys of morphine and cocaine."

"I am glad that those days are behind us," I remarked.

"I too," he confessed, "thanks to your friendship and care for me. Even while I knew the habit to be destructive, it was nonetheless a source of exquisite pleasure. But I am eternally grateful to you for assisting me in my cessation of the habit. If you had never done me any other service, what you performed in this regard would rank you as one of those in this world to whom I owe most."

I was touched that Holmes would regard my actions in this regard in so favourable a light, and told him so.

"No, no, Watson, you did more than your duty as a doctor,

a friend, and as a human being. If you had not done this for me, I do not know what my current state of health or mental capacity might be.

"In any event, I am, as I think you know from experience, a wretched cook." I smiled to myself, remembering some particularly inedible messes that that been the fruits of Holmes' labours in the kitchen. "I do, however, appreciate good food when it is available, and I was lucky enough to be living almost directly above a little restaurant that provided some of the finest examples of the cuisine of Southern Italy, notably Naples, that it has been my good fortune to encounter. Furthermore, and this was much more to the point at the time I am describing, the bill of fare was well within the range of my purse. The owner of the restaurant, who also acted as the sole waiter in the establishment, was one Signor Ricoletti.

"The poor man suffered from a club-foot, but the deformity did not seem to worry him unduly as he hurried about his business of serving the customers in his establishment, though these were few enough, Heaven knows.

"For my part, I found the food to be particularly to my taste, and at one point I found myself taking my evening meal there almost every night. Accordingly, Ricoletti and I struck up a friendship of sorts, and on those all too frequent nights when the flow of custom was not strong, he would often join me at my table after I had finished my meal, and we would talk."

"In what language did you speak?" I asked Sherlock Holmes, knowing him to have a good knowledge of the Italian language.

"Why, that was one of the principal subjects of our converse. His English was not of a degree of fluency that would allow him to express himself with any degree of confidence, and I had a fancy to better my Italian in order to read the works of Tasso. Accordingly, we tutored each other in our respective native tongues. There, was, however, one fly in this ointment of our friendship, if I may term it so."

"The wife whom you termed 'abominable'?"

"Precisely. The term is not too strong to describe her. Usually, I would hesitate to apply such an epithet to a fellow human being, but there really are very few other words – at least in polite usage," he chuckled, "that fully convey her character.

"She was the cook who produced the meals that I enjoyed night after night, and it was a source of wonder to me that a woman of such a nature could be an artist of such a high order. Many is that time that Ricoletti and I would be talking, when I would hear her harsh voice from the kitchen calling to her unfortunate husband. Muttering an apology to me that his wife was calling him away, he would hurriedly rise and make his way to the kitchen, shutting the door behind him. Even the closed door was not sufficient to mask the screeches and shouts, often accompanied by the sounds of crashes and breaking crockery."

"What was she saying or shouting to him?"

Holmes smiled. "My knowledge of the Italian language was not at the stage where I was able to make out the meaning. In any event, the language spoken appeared to be some sort of rustic dialect, and Ricoletti, bless the man's memory, was attempting to teach me a purer form of the language. When these events occurred, I typically waited for between five and ten minutes. If Ricoletti emerged from the kitchen within that time, we would resume our conversation, by mutual unspoken consent not mentioning the events immediately preceding. If, as sometimes occurred, the altercation was extended, I would leave the money owing for my meal on the table, with a sizeable gratuity added, and quietly make my escape."

"Did you ever catch sight of this virago?"

"Certainly, on a number of occasions. Before I had first seen her, I confess that I had pictured her as one of those Italian signoras where middle age has resulted in a certain broadness of beam, and of generally unattractive appearance. Imagine my surprise when I beheld a young slender woman of considerable beauty. I have seen actresses on the stage with less appeal than this woman.

"Indeed, her youth and her appearance led me at first to believe that she was Ricoletti's daughter or some other relative that he had never mentioned. However, this was dispelled immediately she opened her mouth. The accents and the tone were enough to convince me immediately that this was the termagant who summoned her husband so frequently. The voice, and the character that was evident from the merest glance at her face, were at odds with the general beauty of her appearance. I have seldom, if ever, experienced such a discrepancy."

"What was her attitude towards you?"

"Towards me, she displayed a certain amount of coquetry, which was far from being to my taste, I can tell you. Quite apart from any other matters, she was the wife of a man whom I had come to regard as a friend, and I found her frequent pawings at my sleeve, and the unnecessary proximity when conversing with me to be in poor taste, to say the least. I need hardly add that I found her person and character unappealing."

"What was the husband's reaction to this flirtation?"

"I fear the poor man had seen something of this before. He gazed upon these scenes with what I can only describe as a pitying half-smile. I hasten to add that I gave the woman no encouragement on any occasion whatsoever, least of all in front of him."

"To what do you attribute her interest in you, then?"

"Principally, I believe, to the fact that I was a regular customer, who helped provide her and her husband with an income. Also," and here Holmes appeared to be somewhat embarrassed, "I was a younger man in those days, and my appearance was said by some to be approaching handsome. It may be that there was a degree of attraction on her side, but I would not like to state for certain that that was so. Later, I was to ascribe a different reason for her interest, which I will relate in due course.

"In any event, it seemed to me that the interest and the liking for me which was at first apparent disappeared after a few meetings, and indeed, seemed to turn to a positive dislike."

"Such is often the way," I remarked.

"Is that so? I lack your experience in these matters, Watson," he smiled. "In any event, I met the woman perhaps a half dozen of times before poor Ricoletti's life was shattered by a terrible event.

"I was dressing in my rooms in Montague-street, when there was a frantic knocking on my door.

"'Signor Holmes! Signor Holmes!' came the cry, followed, in a quaint mixture of English and Italian, by 'Come quickly and save me. It is terrible news that I have.'

"I replied to Ricoletti, for I recognised his voice immediately, that I would be joining him soon, and I hurriedly threw on the remainder of my clothes. I opened the door to my room, to discover the poor Italian sitting on the top step of the stairs, wringing his hands and moaning.

"'She is dead,' he said, turning a tear-stained face to me, and speaking his quaint mixture of English and Italian, 'and they will say that I killed her. But I did not, Signor. I did not!'

"The vehemence of his denial struck me, and though, as you know, one can never be certain in these matters, it appeared to me to be extremely unlikely that he could be guilty of murder. I extended my hand to him, and bade him rise and tell me more in the comfort of my room, to which I conducted him.

"I sat him in a chair, and poured him a little brandy and water, which he accepted gratefully, and sipped as he told me his story.

"'We had closed the restaurant the previous night and taken ourselves to our bed,' he began.

"'Excuse the impertinence of the question,' I interrupted him, 'but had you and your wife quarrelled earlier?'

"'Ah yes,' he answered me sadly. 'And what an argument. She threw pots and pans at me. See here.' The poor fellow pulled up a sleeve to disclose a livid bruise which was obviously the result of a blow from a hard object. From the shape of the contusion, the implement could quite possibly have been a cooking pan of some kind. 'She shouted and screamed such names as I will not repeat here. Indeed, she shouted so loud that our neighbours called in the police, believing that I was murdering her. But it was not I who was attacking her – it was the other boot on the foot,' he said, in a quaint turn of English phrasing.

"'And the police arrived?'

"'Indeed, there were two of them. I was able to assure them that I was not the attacker, and that my wife was experiencing some of those changes in mood to which women are subject at regular intervals.'

"'You did not, by chance, notice the numbers of the police constables who visited you?'

"'Alas, no.'

"'No matter. May I enquire the nature of the quarrel between you and your wife?'

"He shrugged expressively. 'With women it is always money that comes first, is it not? She insists that I give all the money that we make from our restaurant. I tell her she has it all. She says to me that I am holding back the money from her. I tell her no, and then she starts to shout. And then she throws things at me,' he said, ruefully rubbing his arm. 'Pots and pans and even a knife.'"

"The old story," I said to Holmes. "An attractive woman married to an older husband takes a lover, who demands money as the price of his silence, once he has taken his fun and tired of her."

Sherlock Holmes raised his eyebrows a little at my speech. "You astonish me with your knowledge of these matters, my dear Watson," he said, with that characteristic half-smile of his. "As it happens, my mind was working along similar lines to the ones you have just described, and as discreetly as I could, I asked Ricoletti if he was aware of any friendships outside their marriage which might account for these moods. He denied it, and I believed him. There was in his face nothing but sincerity. I therefore requested him to continue with his story.

"'It is my task to buy the meat and vegetables each morning, and I usually leave the house early in order to procure the finest ingredients at the best price at the market. This morning, I left Bianca in bed asleep. I returned with my purchases not twenty minutes ago, a little after half-past seven. Usually she is awake on my return, but today, no. I go upstairs, and there she is in bed, slain. Blood everywhere, and one of the knives from the kitchen lying beside her head.'

"'She is still there?' I asked him. 'You touched nothing?'

"'Nothing,' he assured me.

"'And you give me your solemn word that you are not responsible for her death.' He looked at me and held my gaze. 'Signor, I swear to you by the Virgin and all the saints that I did not kill her and that I had nothing to do with her death. But who will believe me? I will be hanged for a crime I did not commit,' he wailed.

"'You have given me your word that you did not kill her, and I believe you,' I told him. 'Trust in me, and I will ensure that you never even come to trial.'

"It was heartening to see the man's face clear at my words. One of the joys of my profession is that I am able to restore hope to those who may feel at times that hope has abandoned them. 'Come, let us be off,' I said to him, taking up the bag that contained the tools of my trade.

"On the pavement outside our house, I encountered a constable. 'There has been murder committed in this house,' I said to him, pointing to the restaurant. 'Murder of this man's wife. I have every reason to believe he is innocent, but I feel it is my duty to lay the facts before the police.' As I spoke to the officer of the law, I saw Ricoletti's face turn ashen.

"'Quite right, too, sir,' said the policeman. 'May I ask where you two gentlemen are going now?'

"'Why, I wish to view the body,' I told him.

"'Are you a doctor or something, then, sir?' asked the bobby.

"'My name is Sherlock Holmes,' I told him, and passed him my card. 'I wish you to accompany us, but before we visit the scene of the crime together, I would like you to use your whistle to summon one of your fellow-constables, and inform Inspector Lestrade of Scotland Yard of the incident, requesting him to come here as soon as possible.'

"'I don't know who you think you are, ordering a police officer around like that,' he complained to me.

"'Believe me, if the Inspector finds out you have not cooperated with me on this, you will find yourself in trouble, my lad,' I told him. He looked me up and down, and pulled out his whistle, which he used to summon another constable, to whom he repeated my instructions."

"Could you really have made trouble for the constable?" I asked Holmes curiously. "I am aware that your relationship with Lestrade now is such that you could achieve such a thing, but at that stage in your career would it have been possible?"

Holmes laughed. "It was bluff on my part, Watson. But bluff, when executed with confidence, can prove as effective as any other argument. At any event, the three of us, the constable, Ricoletti, and myself, made our way up the dingy narrow stairs where the dead woman awaited us, shrouded in a ghastly halo of blood on the pillow. From our position by the door, it appeared that her throat had been pierced, and an artery severed.

"'Please do not enter the room,' I ordered the other two, as I dropped to my knees and examined the floor with my lens. It took less than a minute to ascertain that my friend was almost certainly innocent, and I stood up.

"'There's nothing to see, is there, sir?' the constable said to me, with a faint mocking emphasis on the last word. 'Shall we go in now?'

"'It is vital that we all stay out of the room until the Inspector arrives,' I told him, placing myself in the doorway in such a way that he would have to manhandle me in order to enter. In the event, we had not long to wait. Lestrade arrived, with all the signs of a man who has dressed and shaved in a hurry.

"'Good morning, Holmes,' he greeted me, none too affectionately, I admit. 'I trust this was worth my missing breakfast.' He peered into the room. 'Who is she?' he asked brusquely.

"I introduced Ricoletti as the widower, and declared my faith in his innocence. Lestrade grunted at my pronouncement, but invited me to explain myself. 'I am sure you have reasons for your belief,' he said to me.

"Accordingly, I invited Lestrade to examine the floor with me, and I was clearly able to show to him, through an examination of the impressions in the shabby carpet which covered the floor, that a pair of feet had crossed the floor from the door to the bed, and then, stained with blood, had crossed the floor again and gone out of the door. Although the marks of Ricoletti's feet were also visible, they were in a different part of the floor and had been made after the first set, and were strikingly different. There was no doubt in my mind as to the order in which the prints had been made, and I was pleased to see that Lestrade agreed in full with my conclusions, once they had been made clear to him.

"'Very good, Mr. Holmes,' he said. 'I am perfectly prepared to believe that these are the footprints of the man who killed Mrs. Ricoletti. I also observe Mr. Ricoletti's unfortunate deformity in the shape of his club-foot, and accept that it is not he who has made these prints. I will require you to answer some questions, though, Ricoletti. I must say, though, that you do not appear to be overly stricken with grief at your loss, if I may say so.'

"Knowing the relationship between Ricoletti and his wife, I could not resist a smile, which I trust remained inward only, and did not show itself on my face. The widower answered Lestrade frankly, and I believe honestly. 'I cannot truthfully say I am sorry, sir. The woman made my life a misery, and my life, though it will be hard for me to keep the restaurant without her, will be an easier one.'

"'Then you go with the constable here to the station and await my arrival. Mr. Holmes, have you examined the body?'

"'Not at all. Do you want to call the police surgeon?'

"Lestrade waited until the constable was down the stairs before he answered me in a low voice. 'No, Mr. Holmes, I do not. The police surgeon available to me today is a drunken oaf and his assistant is little more than a schoolboy. I believe that you and I are possessed of at least a modicum of common-sense in these matters, so let us examine the wound.'"

"That would seem to be a rather damning indictment of the police surgeon at that time," I said to Holmes.

"It was, I fear, an accurate one at that time. Lestrade's judgement in this particular instance could not be faulted. Matters have improved in that department since then, however. In any event, Lestrade and I moved to the bed, taking care not to disturb, as far as was possible, the footprints noted earlier.

"'Halloa!' I exclaimed, looking at the knife and comparing it to the gory wound in the dead woman's neck. 'This knife is not the murder weapon!'

"'But it is covered in blood,' Lestrade objected.

"'It is not covered,' I pointed out. 'Some blood has somewhat inartistically been daubed on the blade in a way that could never have occurred naturally, in an attempt to make us believe that this is the murder weapon. It is, Ricoletti informed me, a knife from the restaurant kitchen, and was therefore placed here in an attempt to deceive. If further proof is needed, examine the wound, and ask yourself whether this knife could have produced this wound.'

"Lestrade bent over the body and proceeded to examine the corpse. 'You are right. This wound was produced by a stiletto or some such similar knife.'

"'The Italian assassin's traditional weapon,' I reminded

him.

"'A former lover?' suggested Lestrade.

"I shook my head. 'I feel there is something more to it than that,' I said. 'Look here.' By the side of the bed stood a picture of Mary and the Holy Infant. 'That, though you may not know it, Lestrade, is a reproduction of Our Lady of Naples, sometimes known as the Black Madonna. An image which is particularly sacred to those criminal gangs of the city, known collectively as the Camorra.'

"'You think this is a gang killing?' asked Lestrade.

"'I cannot say with certainty without further proof, of course,' I answered, 'but were I a wagering man, I would be almost certain of it.'

"'There are women in these gangs?' asked Lestrade.

"'I believe in some cases, the women are the leaders,' I told him."

"How did you come to know of this?" I asked Holmes.

"My interests, as you know, are wide-ranging, and in this modern age, where honest men so often cross borders, it seemed to me that rogues and villains might also do so. It seemed to me to be expedient to gain at least a superficial knowledge of the malefactors of other countries – the Apaches of Paris, and the banditti of the Latin nations, for example. The Camorra are notorious for the wide range of their activities, as well as the fragmentary nature of their organization.

"In any event, we left the chamber of death and made our way to the police station, where Ricoletti was waiting for us. I decided that there was little or no point in beating about the bush, and I therefore asked him directly, 'Was your wife Bianca in any way connected with the Camorra?'

"'Why, yes,' he replied, looking nervously about him.

"'And you?' Lestrade asked.

"'No, never, I swear it,' he assured us with great

earnestness. 'Listen to me, and I will explain all. It may seem strange to you that I,' and he gestured towards his deformed foot, 'should be united with a woman such as she, who possessed such beauty. But I can tell you that it was not by her choice, nor mine, that we were married.

"'Her father was one of the leaders of a Camorra gang, and Bianca, from an early age, was a wild one, with a temper that would make grown men shake with fear. Because of this, and because of her father's reputation, no man would take her in marriage, despite her good looks. Her father was likewise frightened that she, if allied to another member of the gangs, would seek to overthrow his position.

"'At that time, I was working in a restaurant in Naples where Bianca and her father often visited, and I waited upon them at their table. On one occasion, I was serving them their meal, and they were arguing bitterly. It appeared that Signor Capatelli wished his daughter to enter a convent, I assume as a measure of self-protection, but as you can guess, she would have none of it.

"'"Why, I would sooner marry that cripple there!" she shrieked, pointing at me.

"'"And so you shall," her father said to her. Whereupon, before either she or I could fully grasp the situation, we were married within the week, and her father had bought the restaurant where I was working, and presented it to us as a wedding gift. I do not know how achieved his goal, but he forced Bianca to work in the kitchen, where she transpired to have a real gift as a cook, as you, Signor Holmes, can testify.

"'But she chafed at the marriage and the life of a restaurant, and one day she proposed to me that we move to London, telling me that her father had suggested the move to her, and given her the money, which she displayed to me, to effect the change. I, like a fool, agreed.'

"'Why do you call yourself a fool?' I asked him.

"'Because it was all a lie,' he replied. 'The money had been stolen from her father, who had no knowledge of her intention of moving to London, but I only discovered the truth by chance. We had been here for a short while only, when I was accosted one day by one of my fellow-countrymen, who spoke to me in the rough dialect of the Neapolitan back streets.

"' "We know who you are, and what you have stolen from us," he said to me. I protested that I had no knowledge of what he was saying, and he proceeded to inform me of my wife's crimes. I managed to persuade him of my lack of involvement in the business, but he said to me, "You may be safe from the vengeance of the Camorra, but your wife will never know a day's peace. One day, when she is least expecting it, her father's retribution will pierce her lovely throat like an arrow. It may come tomorrow, or it may come in one year or even longer. But make no mistake, Signor, it will come as surely as the night follows the day."

"'When I returned home, I talked to Bianca, who went deathly pale at the knowledge that her theft had been discovered. From that day on, she became a devil. Her temper became even worse than before, and it was clear to me she was in a constant state of fear that the assassin would find her. And so it transpired, as I discovered this morning.' Ricoletti sat in a posture of defeat, his elbows on his knees, and his head buried in his hands. Lestrade and I looked at each other.

"'It is as good an explanation as any,' Lestrade said to me. 'You have shown me, Mr. Holmes, that this unfortunate is innocent of his wife's murder. And it would seem to me to be a waste of time to go searching for an unknown Italian assassin, who by now is probably safely back on the ship by which he reached these shores.'

"'I agree,' said I. It was now clear to me that the woman had taken an interest in me, not on account of any qualities of my person, but because of my profession. It is quite possible that she had in mind some use for me as a defence of some kind against those she expected, with good reason, to be sent against here.

"Lestrade discharged Ricoletti, whom I never saw again. I heard that he had taken his own life out of despair at the events that had taken place around him. At any event, his clothes were found on the Embankment early one morning, and it was assumed he had drowned himself in the Thames."

"A sad tale, then," I said to my friend. "You saved a man from the gallows, where he would undoubtedly have ended had it not been for you, and yet he took his own life."

"That is so, Watson. Indeed, when I heard of his supposed death, I very nearly gave up the profession I had chosen for myself. What use was I to Society, I asked myself, if all I could achieve was a result of this kind? It took several other cases before I could fully persuade myself that my chosen path was in truth of value to others." Sherlock Holmes sat silently in thought for a full five minutes, and suddenly brightened. "But come, less of this melancholy talk. Let us amuse ourselves by considering in advance the menu of our first meal in the land of the gastronome."

The Adventure of the Two Bottles

"I COULD NOT HELP BUT REMARK THAT THE CHILDREN RAN TO HER ARMS AS READILY AS THEY DID TO THOSE OF THEIR AUNT, AND HER ATTITUDE TOWARDS THEM WAS ALL THAT ANY OBSERVER OF THE DOMESTIC SCENE COULD WISH TO ENCOUNTER."

EDITOR'S NOTES

As Watson notes in The Sign of the Four, Holmes made mention of this case in connection with Miss Mary Morstan, giving some details. In "The Musgrave Ritual", he likewise talks about some early cases, and mentions that "during my last years at the university there was a good deal of talk there about myself and my methods". It seems that the affair of the Gloria Scott was not the only case which the young Holmes handled in his student days, but for some reason, Watson chose not to pass this account on to his agent, Sir Arthur Conan Doyle.

Even so, the case is of considerable interest. It shows the way in which the younger Holmes developed his powers and his techniques of deduction. It also shows a young man more than a little overpowered by the unfamiliar proximity of an attractive woman – a state which we cannot imagine as being one that was often assumed by the mature Holmes. Perhaps it is this last that led Watson to keep it hidden in the dispatch-box. He gave it no title, so I have taken the liberty of naming it "The Adventure of the Two Bottles".

 HAVE frequently mentioned in my accounts of the adventures of Mr. Sherlock Holmes that he was reticent in the extreme about his early life. From time to time he would drop hints about adventures and cases before my acquaintance with him, and I have recounted the details of some of them as he told them to me.

I remember one occasion, though on which he remarked that "the most winning woman I ever knew was hanged for poisoning three little children for their insurance-money". Since it was rare for him to use such terms as "winning" in connection with the fair sex, this remark caused some sparks of curiosity to smoulder within my breast. At that time, they did little more than smoulder, as to be sure, at that time thoughts of my dear Mary occupied my mind to the exclusion of little else save the immediate solution of the case which occupied Sherlock Holmes and myself. However, these words of his remained in my mind for some years and one day, on our return from a case in the country – this was the case at King's Pyland involving the racehorse Silver Blaze – I brought up the subject. We were sitting alone in our first-class compartment, and the wild countryside of Dartmoor had long since been left behind. I had foolishly neglected to procure any reading matter at the station, and Holmes likewise appeared to be somewhat at a loss for mental stimulation, as was frequently the case following the successful resolution of a problem.

" 'Pon my soul, Watson, I would never have expected you to remember that remark of mine that I tossed off so casually so long ago," he exclaimed in answer to my query. " Bravo, my dear chap, bravo indeed. I take it you are all agog to hear the story ? "

I readily assented, and Holmes began to tell his tale. " It

was while I was a student at University*. I had already begun to develop my powers of observation and the faculty of reasoning and drawing deductions from my observations, as I think I have mentioned to you before now. It made of me, as you may well imagine, somewhat of a curiosity among my fellows, and they were continually setting little tests for me, making wagers among themselves as to whether I could solve the problems they set before me.

"In this way, I gained much knowledge and practice through constant and varied exercise of my talents, which would otherwise have cost me many years of everyday experience. I may say with all due modesty that the odds laid against me – that is to say, against my failure to deliver a satisfactory solution – lengthened by the month.

On one day, I was studying, when there was a knock on the door of my rooms, and a student of the same year as I entered. O'Donnell, for that was his name, had a worried expression on his face, and I begged him to sit and compose himself before he spoke. He obeyed, and sat with his head in his hands for a good ten minutes before he raised his face and looked me in the eye."

"You were more patient than I at that age," I laughed. "Why, I cannot imagine sitting in silence with a fellow-student of mine for more than a minute or two at the most."

"Nonetheless, as I have remarked in the past, Watson, you now have now developed the great gift of silence and

---

* Editor's note : Watson never gives the name of the university that Holmes attended. We may be certain that he knew, but for some reason declined to acquaint his readers with the knowledge. My personal opinion is that Holmes attended Trinity College, Dublin, and my reasons are given in a short paper entitled "Was Sherlock Holmes a Catholic ?" published in the *Baker Street Journal* (Vol. 63, No.2, Summer 2013)

calm about you, which is so often a balm to a spirit such as mine. At the time I am describing, I was naturally – nay, I am still – an active restless soul. I was endeavouring to discipline myself into habits of peace and tranquillity, especially when confronted with those in a state of agitation. I find that this often inspires confidence, and encourages my supplicants to speak more freely than would otherwise be the case. After our long unspoken communion, if I may put it in those terms, O'Donnell spoke to me.

"'Holmes, the whole College is well aware of your abilities in that strange field you have named as deduction. My question to you now is whether you are as discreet as you are astute.'"

"What a singularly offensive question!" I exclaimed. "I wonder you did not send him away immediately."

"Not as offensive as you might imagine," replied Holmes. "I confess to having made somewhat of a spectacle of myself in the College, in the hope that this would bring forth further challenges on which I might sharpen my wits, and I dare say that I had something of a reputation as a braggart. However, I had determined that were to exercise these talents for the benefit of others, I would do so with discretion, and would follow a code of conduct similar to that of a lawyer, or a doctor. I therefore provided O'Donnell with the assurance that he required.

"He thanked me, and began his tale. 'It is my stepmother,' he told me. 'My father has recently married again, following the death of my mother some two years ago. I have three younger siblings, two sisters and a brother, much younger than myself, aged eight, seven and five. Recently, my father's new wife, who is only a little older than I, seems to have set herself up against my aunt, my mother's sister.'

"'In what way has she set herself up?' I asked.

" ' One example I can give you, which occurred only a few days ago when I returned to my father's home in County Clare. My sisters and brother were in the nursery. I happened to come out of my room into the passage that leads to the nursery, just as my aunt was passing along on her way to the children. I watched as she knocked on the nursery door, which opened, and to my surprise I saw my stepmother, rather than the nursery-maid I had expected, framed in the entrance. She and my aunt exchanged words in low voices which I was unable to hear clearly, and was unable to make out any words spoken. What happened next utterly astonished me. My stepmother pushed vigorously with both hands against my aunt's chest, causing her to stumble and fall to the ground.

" ' I was in two minds as to whether to come to her rescue, and thereby face my stepmother's possible wrath, or whether to ignore the whole incident. Discretion formed the better part of valour, and I quietly closed the door of my room and determined to forget the incident.

" ' As you can imagine, though, it was hard for me to forget what I had seen, and on my return to College, I determined to seek advice. You, Holmes, must help me to find out what is going on in that house.'

" ' Very well,' I told him. ' But you must answer a few questions for me. I have as yet insufficient data on which I can base any kind of assumptions, let alone reach conclusions. Firstly, how old is your aunt ? The same age as your stepmother ? ' You may remark here, Watson, how I was slowly learning the business of collecting the facts of the case before attempting to bring reason to bear."

" I had noted that," I smiled.

" In any event, I elicited the following: the new Mrs. O'Donnell was approximately the same age as my friend, perhaps one or two years older, but no more than that, while Miss O'Donnell, the older sister of his father, was some twenty-five years older. She lodged with her brother and his family, having never married, and in the interval between my friend's mother's death and his father's remarriage had charge of the children, including my friend.

"'And the relations between her and the children?' I asked him.

"'Excellent,' he replied without hesitation. 'I confess that as a younger man on the verge of maturity (as I saw myself two years ago), I had those disagreements and fallings-out that are common between generations, but she was kindness itself, and any supposed curbs on my freedom were made from a position of concern for my well-being. As for my younger brother and sisters, they quite frankly adored her. She always seemed to have time and a kind word for them.'

"'And your stepmother?' I asked. 'Is she the wicked stepmother of legend?'

"'By no means,' he said, smiling. 'She loves those children as if they were her own. Indeed, I may safely say that she spends more time with them, and appears more deeply attached to them, than my mother when she was alive, if it does not appear too disrespectful to her memory to say so. She was an invalid for the last few years of her life, her constitution having been damaged by her last confinement, and was bed-ridden for much of the time.'

"'And at that time, your aunt assumed her place in the children's to a greater or less degree?'

"'That is so.'

"'Then,' I told him, with all the pomposity and self-assurance of an over-confident young man, 'the reason for the altercation that you witnessed is simple. It is jealousy, and the two women battle, as women do, for the affection of the children.' I see you smiling, Watson, at my glib and overly simple explanation."

"I apologise, Holmes."

"No need, my dear fellow. Indeed, I smile myself at the callow and over-serious young man that I was then. My friend was of the same opinion as you, and smiled sadly. 'If it were that simple a matter, Holmes, I would not have consulted you on the matter. There is much more to this than I have told you. The incident I have just described is but one in a series of somewhat distressing events that have left me sorely perplexed. Only three weeks ago, my sisters and my brother fell ill. Our family physician was unable to ascribe any definite cause to the malady, but gave it as his opinion that the bad air from the nearby bog had caused some sort of weakness in the children's lungs. Though this seemed unlikely to me, I held my peace – I am no expert in medical matters, after all. What was singular, though, were the relations between my aunt and my stepmother. My aunt devoted herself to the care of the children for three consecutive days and nights, and my stepmother never entered the nursery all that time. Only following specific requests from my father did she provide assistance to my brother and sisters, by which time my aunt was in a state of almost total collapse from exhaustion. I am sadly disturbed that my stepmother was not willing to assist my aunt in the nursing duties, given that she claims to be devoted to the children.'

"'Then what you described earlier is doubtless no more than a matter of retaliation on your stepmother's part for what she perceives as a slight and a dereliction of duty,' I retorted. 'My original thesis still stands. There is no more to this than a struggle over the children's affection.'

"'Be that as it may,' he replied. 'I came with an invitation to spend a few days as a guest with us, so that you may see for yourself the state of affairs, and to observe the characters of the principals.'

" 'Very well,' I told him, nothing loath to this proposal. The study on which I was engaged was not to my taste, and there was little or no urgency involved. We agreed a date on which I should visit Dunsany House, the family home."

I smiled to myself at Holmes' description of his academic labours, knowing as I did his somewhat extraordinary depth of understanding in various fields of human study, coupled with what I can only describe as an abysmal lack of knowledge in so many others, as I have described elsewhere.

"Accordingly," Holmes continued, "we set out on the appointed day. As always in that part of the world, the weather was grey and damp, and it was a pair of cold, rather wet, and somewhat dejected young men who rang the bell at the front door of Dunsany House†.

" Once inside, we were treated to a warm welcome. It was obvious that whatever the relations between my friend's aunt and his stepmother, an enviably close feeling existed between the other members of the family. The warmth with which the son was received was extended to his guest, and before long I almost felt myself to be one of the family, dressed in dry clothes, and taking my ease before a roaring fire, a glass of the local whiskey beside me.

"The young children were charming young things— You wished to say something, Watson ? "

"It is nothing, Holmes. It is simply that it is the first time I have ever heard you describe young children as being 'charming'."

---

†   Editor's note : This mention of the weather, and the fact that no mention is made of a sea voyage to a location in Ireland adds further support to my belief that Sherlock Holmes' university education took place at Trinity College, Dublin.

" I am not quite the inhuman calculating machine that on occasion you have accused me of being," he said, with a smile. "Though as you are well aware, marriage and a family are not for me, it does not mean that I am unable to appreciate those of others, and it was a positive pleasure to be in what appeared to be such a congenial family atmosphere. It was hard for me to reconcile what I had been told by O'Donnell with what I was experiencing."

"And what did you observe about the aunt and the step-mother?" I could not help but ask.

"All in good time, Watson. Let me first describe the other principals in the case. You see," and his eyes twinkled, " I am not averse to adopting some of the dramatic methods that you adopt when you recount our little adventures. My fellow-student first, Kevin O'Donnell. A pleasant enough fellow, and we knew each other slightly from a common interest in fencing. My weapon is the foil, as you know, and his was the sabre, so we rarely faced each other on the piste, but we were on more than merely nodding terms. His father was typical of his class – a man of more heart than brain, I would have to say, but conscious of the duties that were incumbent upon one of his estate, and mindful of his tenants' needs.

"The children I just described as being charming, and that word is one which fits them well. They were almost unnaturally quiet during the time in the room with us, a state which I ascribed to the unknown illness that they had recently suffered. In my experience, children of that age typically exhibit more curiosity, and are of a more boisterous nature than were these. However, they all, with a solemnity that was almost comical, approached me and made a bow or a curtsey, according to sex, and introduced themselves. Daisy, the eldest, with an enchanting little smile, Mary, the next, was grave and sober in her introduction, as was Dermot, the little boy.

And now to the two principals in the case, as I had already begun to think of them. First, the aunt. She was most unprepossessing in appearance, being afflicted with a severe torticollis, or wryneck, and also with a squint. However, once these disabilities had been overlooked, there was nothing but kindness in the face, and also in the words and voice with which she welcomed me as a friend of her nephew. It was clear, that as O'Donnell had told me, she was adored by the children. However, their affections were obviously divided. The stepmother struck me at first glance as being little better than some of the women one sees around Piccadilly of an evening. Young, as I had been told, and undeniably possessed of a particular form of attractiveness, she was dressed in a provocative fashion that left few of her charms to the imagination. She formed a striking contrast to the aunt, who was clad in a sombre and sober style. I lack your skill in the description of female attire, Watson, so I will content myself with this meagre account.

"Even before she had opened her mouth, I confess that I had prejudged the woman as a vulgar fortune-hunter. Her first words of welcome to me acted to dispel that impression. The voice was low and cultured, and the words were carefully chosen to put me at my ease. You must remember that my hostess was a mere two or three years older than I, and my experience with the female sex to that date had been largely confined to the members of my family. In any event, it was a novel, thrilling, and somewhat unnerving experience for me to be confronted by this apparition. I confess to not being totally unmoved by her attentions, and by the way that she placed herself close to me when she addressed me. My unease was further accentuated by her heady perfume which swam in my nostrils.

"Notwithstanding all of this, I could not help but remark

that the children ran to her arms as readily as they did to those of their aunt, and her attitude towards them was all that any observer of the domestic scene could wish to encounter. From what I could observe, there was no forcing of affection on either side, and the caresses bestowed and received on all sides were sincerely given and accepted.

"However, there was no escaping the fact that when a child ran from the arms of the aunt to those of the stepmother, or vice versa, a look of dislike often shot from the abandoned party to the new receiver of the child's affection. Such looks seemed to be stronger when directed from the older woman to the younger, but that may have been merely a result of my fancy, since Miss O'Donnell's squint gave many of her facial expressions an evil cast.

"I could discern nothing which would account for the incident that had been recounted to me other than a competition for the children's affections, and in the relatively remote location of the house, it would be easy to see how such a rivalry could take on an exaggerated form which could lead to acts of violence such as had been described.

"After some time, the nursery-maid arrived to collect the children and to take them to their tea, whereupon I addressed myself to the aunt.

"'I believe the children have been unwell recently?' I asked, in the hope of gaining a little insight into the matter. My intention was also to bring the stepmother into the conversation in the hope that I might observe the interchanges between the two women. I may as well remark that at this point my host, my friend's father, had left the room.

"My words had an immediate effect on the stepmother, despite their being addressed to the aunt. The younger woman's face took on a stony expression, and there was a determined set to her lips which indicated an inner resolve of which she did not seem capable at first sight.

"'Why, yes, Mr. Holmes,' the aunt replied in answer to my question. 'The poor little things were quite unwell for a number of days. The doctor put it down to the bad air that emanates from the countryside around here.'

"I was just about to remark that I had been told this, when the younger woman spoke. 'With all due respect, Miss O'Donnell,' she said, in a voice that had nothing of respect in it, 'the doctor is a fool.'

"'You should know better than to speak of your elders in that fashion, Kathleen,' replied the aunt, in a tone that was as cold as that of her interlocutor. The words brought a flush to the young wife's cheek, but she bit her lip and said nothing in reply.

"I quickly attempted to step into the breach. 'What exactly were the symptoms?' I asked, addressing myself to the aunt.

"'Why, are you a medical student, Mr. Holmes?' she asked me, all traces of her anger now seemingly vanished. I gave some noncommittal answer, and she proceeded to tell me of the circumstances surrounding the children's illness.

"'All three of them woke up in the morning with headaches, and complaining of tiredness and weakness. I did all I could for them that morning, but by lunch-time it was clear that there was nothing more that I could do, and so I sent for our Dr. Flanagan, who came immediately. He took the pulse of all of them, and declared that the life of poor little Dermot, being the youngest and the smallest of them, was in some danger. He prescribed cold compresses and tonics for all of them, and a special tonic for Dermot. I sat with them night and day for three days until I, too, was forced to take to my bed.'

"I made suitable noises of sympathy, as the memory of

that time had brought tears to her eyes, which she dabbed with a handkerchief. 'I am sorry, Mr. Holmes,' she said to me through her tears. 'The memory is yet painful. I trust you will excuse my leaving you now.' I stood, and escorted her to the door. My friend O'Donnell and I were now alone in the room with the young Mrs. O'Donnell, who addressed herself to my friend.

"'Kevin,' she said to him, and I noted the free and unaffected use of the Christian name as a form of address, 'I appear to have left my book upstairs. It is an edition of Dickens' *The Tale of Two Cities*, in a green binding. You will find it beside my bed.'

"He assented, and left the room. 'I assume, Mrs. O'Donnell,' I remarked, 'that you wish to speak with me alone, since I see the book beside you on the seat of your armchair.'

"She laughed gaily, and leaned forward to pat my arm, but there was a look of some wariness in her eyes. 'Why, Mr. Holmes,' she said. "You miss very little, do you? Very well, I will tell you quickly what I want you to know. The doctor is indeed a fool. I know what I speak of. My father was a doctor himself, and a good one. You see me dressed and painted like this and no doubt you have marked me down as a fortune-hunter. Ha, yes, I see your face. You need not blush for yourself, as almost everyone makes the same assumption when they meet me. I dress and appear like this because it gives great pleasure to Mr. O'Donnell, whom I genuinely love with all my heart and respect as a generous and full-hearted gentleman. It pleases me to please him in this way. But I am no brainless painted mannequin, Mr. Holmes. I have a head on my shoulders as good as that of most men.'

"When I heard these words, I felt ashamed of my earlier judgements, Watson. There seemed to me to be an absolute sincerity in her speech."

"Perhaps you were still influenced by her perfume and her attire?" I suggested.

"There may have been a little of that," he confessed, "but I could not help but consider her to be sincere, callow youth though I may have been at that time. She continued her narrative. 'The doctor, as I say, is a fool. The illness that they suffered was nothing like that caused by the bad air from swamps and bogs. When Charlotte O'Donnell took to her bed after her extended spell of nursing, I moved into the nursery, and there was an immediate improvement, within two or three hours of my assuming the nursing duties. Within two days, the three children were all fit and healthy once more.'

"'Why did you not relieve Miss O'Donnell in her nursing duties earlier?' I asked.

"'I was not permitted to do so,' she replied. 'I offered to do so, as anyone in the house will bear witness, but there was no question of her deserting her post, as she termed it. I offered my assistance several times, but to no avail.' You will note, Watson, that this account differed significantly in the interpretation of the facts from that I had previously been given by my friend. It was an early lesson to me that it is not the facts alone that may have significance, but also the interpretation that may be placed on those facts by those involved.

"'And your husband's reaction to all this?' I asked her.

"'My dear David's devotion to his sister is life-long. The two of them have been together for almost the whole of their lives. I do not pass judgement on her in front of him and I try, as far as is possible within my power, to avoid crossing her in front of him.'

"She looked into my eyes and took my hand in hers. 'Mr. Holmes, I do not know who you are, or yet what manner of man you may be. But I fear for those little ones, Mr. Holmes, and my fear does not yet have a name. But in God's name, sir, help us and drive this evil, whatever it may be, from this house.'

"My blood fairly chilled, Watson, when I heard these words spoken by this woman. Her pressure on my hand increased as she continued gazing into my eyes. I cannot tell what might have transpired had not footsteps sounded outside the door of the room. She released my hand and sat back in her chair as O'Donnell entered.

"'I am sorry, Kevin,' his stepmother said to him as he approached her chair empty-handed, 'but I discovered the book here beside me a minute or so after you had left us. I do apologise for wasting your time in that way.'

"He did not appear to be unnecessarily put out by this, and turned to me. 'The rain seems to have cleared up a little, Holmes,' he said. 'Shall we go out and look at the horses?'

"And so I was left with a pretty little puzzle to solve. There was no doubt in my mind that there was some mystery, and that mystery was connected with the recent illness of the children. It was equally clear to me that I was dealing with two women of strong will, at least one of whom was also possessed of a formidable intelligence.

"I questioned O'Donnell, as casually as I was able, regarding the finances and the estate of the household. From him I learned that the O'Donnell line had become impoverished relatively recently, following the death of my friend's grandfather, whose death had exposed a number of large gaming debts that he had kept hidden from his family, and the repayment of which had led to a significant diminution of the family's assets. Let that be a lesson to you, Watson," he admonished me with a wagging finger. "You have just seen for yourself at King's Pyland what evils are occasioned through gambling."

"My dear Holmes—" I began indignantly, and broke off, realising that I was being " chaffed" gently by my friend.

"Very well, then. However, the family appeared to be living in fine style, and this was explained by O'Donnell by the fact that his late mother had inherited a most substantial fortune from her parents. This money was sufficient to maintain the handsome establishment in which we now found ourselves, including the horses in the stables. It was clear to me that a few of these were not the cobs and hacks that usually grace a country squire's stables, and appeared to be prime hunters.

"'A crochet of my aunt's,' explained O'Donnell. 'Though she does not ride to hounds herself, she prides herself as a judge of horseflesh, and maintains this stable of steeplechasers which are ridden in races up and down the country.'

"'Do they win?' I asked, curious.

"O'Donnell shook his head. 'I fear not,' he smiled. 'It does not prevent Aunt Charlotte from continuing in her attempts. My father is very generous in his funding of her activities.' He smiled.

"'Has she inherited your grandfather's tendency towards wagering? Forgive me for asking, but if you require my assistance in clearing up this matter, I really feel that I must know these things.'

"The smile left his face. 'I fear so. My father has perhaps been too generous in the past. When he married again, I believe that my stepmother persuaded him to curb his expenses in this direction. But to the best of my knowledge, my aunt continues to wager on the horses.'

"So you see, Watson, I now had another reason to believe in the enmity between aunt and stepmother. I had not the authority nor, to be frank, the inclination to delve into the financial affairs of this family, but it struck me that such an investigation would reveal a flow of money away from the beloved sister, and into the fashionably attired pockets of the new wife. I said as much to O'Donnell, and added the affections of the children as an additional reason for the hostility that obtained between the women of that household.

"'You are right, I suppose,' he said, when I had given my explanation. 'But you have seen my stepmother. She is not constantly grasping after money.'

"Yes, I thought to myself, but to attire oneself in the fashions of the day as did Kathleen O'Donnell – again, Watson, I lack your eye and experience in such matters – appeared to me to be a habit that could not be conducted cheaply. Perhaps her doting husband allowed her sufficient funds to indulge her whims.

"We returned to the house, to be greeted by Miss O'Donnell, who fixed me with her squinting eye, her wryneck turned in my direction.

"'Mr. Holmes,' she greeted me with cordiality. 'I trust you will not think too ill of me for retiring just now. The truth is that I have a very sensitive heart, and the thought of those poor little mites suffering brought back painful memories which I would sooner be without. I am somewhat ashamed of my actions. Put them down, if you will, to a nature which is too generous.' She spoke these words in a soft, but urgent voice, which lent sincerity to her words. "And pray,' she added, 'forget those words of mine spoken to Kathleen. She has a good heart and means well. At the time of the children's illness, we were both under a severe strain, and I fear that neither of us has completely recovered from it.'

"It was a pretty little speech, Watson, and the tones were convincing, as were the words. And yet... and yet I knew not what I should make of it. There was something very appealing about this older woman, despite her deformities, and even knowing as I did of her tendency to gamble, I could not help but be attracted to the seeming simplicity of character that she displayed. And at the same time, there was something that burned in my mind – the words of the younger woman, imploring me to help the children against some unnamed force of evil. I found it impossible to believe in such a source of evil in that household when I examined those with whom I was dealing.

"When my conversation with Miss O'Donnell was over, I told my friend O'Donnell once more that in my opinion, the rivalry between the two women was a matter of a battle for the affections of the younger children, as well as possibly for O'Donnell himself (for I had observed both of them shooting tender glances in his direction), and exacerbated by the dispute over money that had been alluded to. I therefore proposed that I should return to college at the earliest opportunity, but O'Donnell refused any such idea, insisting that I remain with the family for at least another two days.

"Accordingly, I did as he proposed, continuing to observe the family and drawing whatever conclusions I could from these observations. The older Mr. O'Donnell continued to recommend himself to me as one of the better specimens of his type, and his sister likewise, following the one outburst I have described, revealed herself to be one of the sweetest women I have ever encountered. The young Mrs. O'Donnell continued to fascinate me, though, not merely by the allure of her physical presence, intoxicating as it was to a young man, but also by the quality of her mind, which showed itself in opinions regarding politics and other similar subjects, in which she expressed herself with an almost masculine grasp of the topics under discussion. I noticed, however, that she did not exhibit these characteristics while Miss O'Donnell was in the room.

"Not once during the remainder of my stay did she allude

verbally to our earlier *tête-à-tête* until the day of our departure. As O'Donnell and I were mounting into the trap, she seized my hand and pressed it warmly, murmuring in a voice that only I could hear, 'Do not forget what I told you earlier. The lives of three innocents may depend on it.'

"These words rang in my ears on the journey back to the University. I had no conception of the danger to which she was referring, and yet I believed that I could not have been more observant, and that I had missed nothing of importance during my visit. Had something been so closely thrust under my nose that I was unable to see it?

"You must know the feeling, Watson, when you have spent hours of patient work examining minutiae, only to discover that the one datum which provides the solution to the mystery has loomed so large that it has become invisible."

"Indeed I do," I replied. "It is a fault to which doctors, as well as others, are often prone."

"In any event, I was unable to discern whatever it was that was under my nose. I saw little of O'Donnell for the next few weeks, as examinations were approaching, but one day he burst into my rooms, with a wild expression on his face.

"'Holmes!' he exclaimed. 'You must come with me now. They are all dead! Dead, I tell you!'

"'Calm yourself,' I said to him. 'Who are dead?'

"'My brothers and my sisters! All three at a stroke!'

"As you may imagine, I was instantly all ears, and begged him for details, while supplying him with a glass of whiskey and water, of which he seemed in need. Between his sips, he gave me to understand that, starting about a week from when we left Dunsany House, the children had fallen ill. I remembered that on the previous occasion, it had been reported that the children had recovered when their stepmother had taken charge of the sick-room, following three days of nursing by the aunt. I therefore asked him who had charge of the children. And what, Watson, do you think was his answer?"

"I can hardly tell you," I replied. "I would assume, based on past experience, that the children took ill while the aunt was in charge of their care, and recovered when the step-mother relieved her. Presumably, being a doctor's daughter, she has some medical knowledge, if no formal training, and is therefore better placed to alleviate the symptoms of any childish maladies."

"That was my first assumption, too. To my surprise, O'Donnell told me that the exact opposite was true. The aunt had departed for a race meeting in the south of the coun-try when the children suddenly fell sick with the same symp-toms as before. The stepmother nursed them devotedly, but seemingly to no avail. On her return, having been summoned by telegram, the aunt took on the duties of a nurse, and the children recovered."

"But you told me just now that O'Donnell informed you of their deaths?" I objected.

Holmes smiled. "So he did. Hear me out, as I was forced to hear out O'Donnell. Believe it or not, an identical event happened some ten days later. The aunt was away from the house, the children fell sick, and recovered once more when Miss O'Donnell returned. On a third occasion, another stee-plechase meeting claimed the aunt's attention. Once more the children fell ill, a telegram was dispatched, but the aunt failed to return, and the children died."

"It all would appear to be highly suspicious," I said. "It would seem that the return of the aunt was the first step in the children's recovery, after they had fallen ill when only the stepmother was able to take charge. I would suspect some sort of foul play, and the fact that Mrs. O'Donnell is the daughter of a doctor would argue in favour of some sort of poisoning."

"You think exactly as I thought," said Holmes, with an enigmatic smile. "I therefore lost no time in throwing a few necessities into a Gladstone bag and making my way to Dunsany House with my friend.

"We arrived to a grief-stricken house. The faces of both the stepmother and the aunt were furrowed with tears, which flowed freely as they welcomed us to the house. The father showed less emotion on the surface, but it was obvious from his demeanour that he had suffered a crushing blow.

"I enquired as to whether a coroner's inquest had been called, and discovered that no such formality had been undertaken. The doctor had signed the death certificates, giving some fatuous cause such as 'bad air' for the demise of the children. I swiftly determined that the symptoms of the disease that had carried them off were the same as had been observed on the previous occasions, including the illness suffered before my first visit to the house – that is to say, an extreme lassitude accompanied by shooting pains throughout the limbs, starting in the extremities of the fingers and toes, and working their way towards the heart."

"It would definitely appear to have been some sort of poisoning," I said to Holmes. "I would have to consult a pharmacopœia to determine the exact toxin involved, but it sounds like no disease of which I am aware."

"I had come to the same conclusion, and I therefore cast about for the source of the poison. I requested and obtained permission of Mrs. O'Donnell to question the servants regarding the food that was served to the children immediately before and during their illnesses. My intention, which I then proceeded to carry out, was to question both Mrs. and Miss O'Donnell on the same matter, and to note any discrepancies between their stories, and those of the servants. It may be noted, by the way, that while Miss O'Donnell was well known to the servants, and appeared to be universally respected and admired by them, the young Mrs. O'Donnell, though less familiar to them, had already inspired much of the same feeling among the domestics. Both, in other words, were seen as women of whom bad words were rarely spoken. I had had an idea that the intuition of servants, who are often more willing to speak freely than their masters and mistresses, would serve me in this instance, but it was not to be. Indeed, Miss O'Donnell's personal maid, who had been in her service for thirty years, seemed to be as devoted to the young mistress of the house as to her older employer.

"I then made my way to the doctor, who lived on the other side of the village, to enquire what medicines he had prescribed. I found him to be much as I had pictured him – a dirty, slovenly, half-drunk man, who appeared to have forgotten the little science that he had ever learned. The patent pills that he had prescribed appeared to me to be little more than placebos, and seemed to contain nothing that would account for the symptoms described, if the label on the bottle that he showed me was indeed accurate.

"'I swear by these things,' he told me. 'Children, young wives, old maids, they can all benefit from them, to be sure. Why, old Miss O'Donnell has swallowed fair hundreds of them in her time.'

"'Has she indeed?' I asked, and was assured that this was so.

"My only conclusion was that Mrs. O'Donnell was a consummate actress, and had somehow introduced poison into the children's food while pretending to nurse them and to demonstrate her devotion to them. Of the composition of the poison, and the actual method by which it was administered,

I was as yet unsure, but I was confident that I knew the perpetrator and the broad strokes by which the crime had been accomplished."

"But to what end?" I could not help asking.

"That was another area in which I had to confess my ignorance. It was, I supposed, possible that the family fortune was at stake in some way, but given the youth of the children, and the fact that my friend was the eldest son, it did not seem that there would be any significant gain to be enjoyed by doing away with the younger children.

"I now had to tread with extreme caution. It was not then, and indeed would not be now, a pleasant task for me to accuse one's hostess of the murder of three young children. You smile, Watson, but I can assure you that it was no laughing matter. Somehow I had to discover the evidence that would confirm my suspicions. My chance came the very next day, when Mr. and Mrs. O'Donnell, together with Miss O'Donnell, were invited to a dinner at a neighbouring house, given by friends who wished to express their sympathy for the family's recent loss. My college friend was to accompany them, and beseeched me to accompany him as a friend of the family, but I declined on the grounds that the occasion was to be a family affair, and I, as one outside the family circle, would be superfluous.

"I therefore had the run of the house, and I accordingly made my way, unobserved, to Mrs. O'Donnell's bed-room and dressing-room, reasoning that this would be the most likely repository for any apparatus and materials that she had used to accomplish her ends. To my surprise, I discovered nothing following a search of the chambers. I have since refined the methods that I use to conduct such searches, but even at this early stage in my career, I can safely say that my technique was far in advance of the police of the day. It was, of course, possible that she had hidden the poison elsewhere, or even disposed of it altogether, but I closed the door of the bed-room behind me, somewhat baffled and frustrated by my failure.

"It occurred to me that, unlikely as it might be, I should extend the same courtesy to Miss O'Donnell. The scientific approach, if nothing else, demanded no less. And there it was, Watson, that I came across something that turned my previous suppositions on their head. It was a piece of paper, bearing three names – the names of the dead children – and headed by the name of a well-known City insurance company. It was a letter advising Miss Charlotte O'Donnell of the fact that a considerable sum of money would be paid to her, through the medium of her bankers, following the demise of the three children. I was thunderstruck by this. In my limited experience, I had never heard of an uncle or an aunt insuring the lives of their nephews and nieces, and certainly not for the considerable sums listed on the paper. It is no exaggeration when I tell you that the money would have maintained a respectable family for several years.

"I now had a motive for murder, but the motive was of the woman I had least suspected of the crime. I now cast about the room and discovered a very interesting collection. Two bottles of those diabolical pills, which were to be expected, given what I had been told by the doctor, but also a blue bottle of white powder, clearly marked "POISON". The bottles of pills were arranged in what appeared to be a deliberate fashion ; one by the poison bottle, and the other at some distance from it. Here I should perhaps explain that the pills themselves were of the type where the drug is enclosed in a gelatine capsule which may be pulled apart and re-closed, after, perhaps, some other substance has been introduced using a spill or some such implement.

"I reasoned that the pill bottle by the poison bottle contained capsules that had been laced with the poison, while the other was innocent. I therefore secreted the suspect bottle in my pocket, and made my way to the stables. There, I came across one of the stable cats, and forced three of the capsules down its throat."

"Holmes! I am disgusted by such wanton cruelty to a dumb animal," I expostulated.

He smiled ruefully. "It was in a good cause, I told myself, and in any event, the beast repaid me for any discomfort, in the form of the wild bites and scratches it inflicted on me. It was not my intention to cause the death of the animal, in any case. I watched to see if there would be any effect, but instant poisons, as you know, are more a matter of romance than they are of reality. However, I judged that such a poison would probably take effect by the next morning.

"I now had the motive and the means. And since she was in the sick-room, she had the opportunity to administer the fatal doses."

"But," I objected, "if I recall correctly, the children's condition worsened when the aunt was absent and only improved when she was present."

"That is very true, and it definitely gave me pause for thought. But then a possible solution occurred to me in the night as I lay awake, ruminating. What if, I asked myself, my adversary here was more subtle than I had previously imagined? If, for example, she had managed to introduce a little poison into the children's food prior to her leaving the house, so that they fell ill, and then arranged, with her devoted servant, to exchange the bottle of pills that the doctor was sure to prescribe for the invalids with the bottle she had previously prepared? When summoned to return, the harmless nostrums would take the place of the poisoned medicine, and the children would recover. The inference to any observer would be clear ; that is, that the older woman had saved the life of the children from the wiles of the young wife."

" But the first occasion ? "

"That, I concluded, was an experiment in dosage. Since the aunt alone was with the children, we do not know how serious their condition actually was on that occasion, and it was my surmise that the time had been spent attempting to discover the dosage which would do a minimal amount of permanent damage to the children's health, while giving the impression that they were seriously ill. The next two occasions were deliberate attempts to place the blame on another, while at the same time raising the status of the actual culprit and helping to establish her innocence with regard to the matter."

"A truly diabolical plot, Holmes," I exclaimed.

"Indeed. I turned over and went to sleep, waking early. I made my way to the stables, and discovered that the cat was apparently suffering from the effects of its involuntary medication the previous evening, though you will be pleased to hear the effects did not appear to be too serious. I now determined to confront Bridget, the maid to Miss Charlotte O'Donnell. I encountered her in the servants' hall, and much to her surprise, bade her come with me where we could talk without being overheard. I confronted her with my theories, with all the force and vehemence of which I was capable, and was gratified to have her confess, in tears, that my suspicions were true. She had been promised, she told me, a tidy sum of money for her part in the crime, which she had taken part in for fear of being turned out with a bad reference.

"I was now happy with my results. As I walked into the dining-room, I had in my pockets two bottles of these wretched pills, one as they had been delivered, and one which had suffered the attentions of Miss O'Donnell. I walked to the place at the table where she was sitting, and stood in such a way that she could not ignore my presence.

" 'Mr. Holmes, a very good morning to you,' she said with a sweet smile that could have melted the heart of a stone.

" 'I fear you are a little fatigued after last night's visit to your friends,' I said.

" 'Why, a little, perhaps,' she acknowledged.

" 'Perhaps one of these pills would be of some benefit to your health,' I said, pulling out one of the bottles – the unaltered one.

" 'Why, how did you know that I took that medicine?' she asked, a little taken aback.

" 'Or perhaps the pills from this bottle?' I said, taking the other from my pocket. Her face turned white.

" 'Where did you find those?' she asked, suddenly angry. 'I demand to know. And what do you mean by this farce?'

" 'Why Charlotte,' said her brother from his place at the head of the table. 'The young man's only having a bit of fun.'

" 'This is no fun for me,' she snapped.

" 'Nor was it fun for Daisy, Mary, and Dermot,' I answered her.

" 'All colour had now drained from her face. 'So you know all?' she gave out in a hoarse whisper.

" 'I believe I do. Bridget has just confirmed to me what I deduced last night.'

" 'Why... why...' but she got no further. Young Mrs. O'Donnell stepped between us, and slapped the older woman hard about the face before moving behind her and pinioning her arms in a manner that would have done credit to a police officer.

" 'You foul murderer!' she spat at the older woman.

" 'What in the world is going on here?' demanded her

husband. I briefly gave the facts of the matter as I understood them, and his face turned ashen. 'Is this true, Charlotte?' he asked his sister, who gave no answer, but nodded dumbly, the tears falling silently down her cheeks. 'Then there is nothing to be done,' he said, and rang the bell for a footman, to whom he gave orders to fetch the police.

"The wretched woman was escorted from the house, weeping. I next saw her in the dock when I was called to give evidence at her trial for murder. It transpired that she had been a major beneficiary in her brother's will following the death of his first wife. Not expecting him to marry again, she had borrowed heavily – gambling again, Watson, you see," and the finger wagged once more in my direction, "on a *post obit* basis, expecting to repay on the death of her older brother."

"And then her plans were thwarted by the arrival of the new wife?"

"Precisely. The new wife had to be disposed of, and some money raised quickly, as it seems the creditors were snapping at her heels. She decided to use the same action to achieve both ends. By taking out insurance on her nephew and nieces, she could assure herself of the benefits should they die, and if she could somehow contrive to cast the blame on her rival, as she saw Kathleen O'Donnell, her other purpose could be realised.

"The system of dosing and recovery was carried out as I had deduced. The servant was bribed and threatened into acting as an accessory. Given the hideous nature of the crimes and the tender age of the victims, the jury did not even need to retire before announcing their verdict and their sentence."

"And the result?" I asked, though I knew the answer.

"She was hanged," he said briefly, and there was silence in our compartment for a number of minutes as the train slowed. "Ah, here we are at Paddington," he remarked, as our journey ended. "Let us hurry. Sarasate plays at the Windsor Hall at half past three, and it is close on the hour now."

IF YOU ENJOYED THESE STORIES…

YOU may enjoy some other adventures of Sherlock Holmes by Hugh Ashton, who has been described in *The District Messenger*, the newsletter of the Sherlock Holmes Society of London, as being "one of the best writers of new Sherlock Holmes stories, in both plotting and style".

Volumes published so far include:

Tales from the Deed Box of John H. Watson M.D.
More from the Deed Box of John H. Watson M.D.
Secrets from the Deed Box of John H. Watson M.D.
The Darlington Substitution (novel)
Notes from the Dispatch-Box of John H. Watson M.D.
Further Notes from the Dispatch-Box of John H. Watson M.D.
The Death of Cardinal Tosca (novel)
The Last Notes from the Dispatch-Box of John H. Watson, M.D.
The Trepoff Murder (ebook only)
1894
Some Singular Cases of Mr. Sherlock Holmes
The Lichfield Murder
The Adventure of Vanaprastha (ebook only)

There are also children's detective stories, with beautiful illustrations by Andy Boerger (who produced the illustrations for this volume), the first of which was nominated for the prestigious Caldecott Prize:

Sherlock Ferret and the Missing Necklace
Sherlock Ferret and The Multiplying Masterpieces
Sherlock Ferret and The Poisoned Pond
Sherlock Ferret and the Phantom Photographer
The Adventures of Sherlock Ferret

Full details of all of these and many more at:
https://HughAshtonBooks.com